Corona Corner:
Impact of Covid-19 on Our Lives

Dr Sudhir Kumar

Corona Corner: Impact of Covid-19 on Our Lives

8/15, Mazda Deluxe Homes, Tank Road,
Off: Alandi Road, Yerwada, Pune 411006
Contact No. +91 8956806072, +91 9665020206
E-mail: drsk22@gmail.com

Published by:
Kindle Direct Publishing

Price: USD 8

(2021)

Disclaimer

This is purely a work of fiction. Unless otherwise indicated, all the names, characters, businesses, places, events and incidents in this book are either the product of the author's imagination or used in a fictitious manner. Any resemblance to actual persons, living or dead, or actual events is purely coincidental. Certain long-standing institutions, agencies, and public offices are mentioned, but the characters involved are wholly imaginary. The opinions expressed are those of the characters and should not be confused with that of the author.

Preface

The sudden urge to write is unexplainable. More than a year has passed since coronavirus was first detected. Quickly changing unprecedented events during Lockdown 1.0 to Lockdown 5.0 and then Unlock 1.0 to Unlock 5.0 have affected all facets of our lives. Right from the toddlers to very senior citizens - all have experienced the impact of the epidemic with idiosyncrasy of their lives. The emotive human beings were unable to express their perplexity and duality of existence. Man's growing instinct of being unconquerable has got a beating to the core. Freedom to fly was encroached by clipping the wings of desire. That resulted in unusual behaviors and multipronged repercussions, therefore.

I have been wondering recently whether this will be forgotten in the history as a passing chapter or will it be etched in our minds as a permanent scar. Maybe the coming generations will forget the present soft-but-impinging sufferings, as we have forgotten today our martyrs of independence struggle. Nevertheless, the ordeals that we have gone through must be penned down somewhere at least for the sake of record and for the benefit of our future generations. For me, there was an option to record all the events as a technical commentary acknowledging electronic and print media. Then it could have been like a journal read by a few interested researchers. However, the message should reach the masses. A common man is more interested in, and loves to read - Stories. And I am the master in telling stories. That's how this fiction was born, which is a combination of facts, imaginations and emotions. It's also a warning of similar extremes that may occur in future and we might be caught napping. The story is told in a common man's style. I am sure you will love it.

PUNE, 2021
THE AUTHOR

Dedicated to

My caring, sharing and loving wife Sandhya.
Your mere presence makes me feel assured.
Friend, philosopher, guide and what not.
Even tranquilizers fail before you.
And yes,
thanks for forgiving your forgetful husband always.

Who killed the killers?

It was one of the lazy afternoons. I woke up with the clattering sound of some equipment being shifted by a nurse. I was admitted in the outer ward of the famous hospital of the city namely "Corona Corner" situated at the end of the deserted road. Eight days ago, I had developed symptoms of cough and cold with some chest congestion. As a precautionary measure, it was advisable to get myself checked up and get tested for Covid-19. Good that we had a hospital nearby. This was a private hospital and was supposed to have high class facilities with modern equipment and hence was chosen by my family. I was pleasantly surprised by the sincerity with which the staff of the hospital attended me. My family was kept outside. After paying the advance cheque they were told to go back home. They were told that my health status would be reported to them on WhatsApp with updates every morning and evening. My Covid test report was still awaited. My health was improving day by day but the doctors were still not sure whether I was really corona positive or not, hence they kept me under observation as they did not want to take risk. On third day morning, the report was expected and I was happy that I would be released soon considering my improving situation. To my great surprise, they showed me my report - positive. I had a serious doubt, hence told the visiting doctor to recheck it. The doctor started shouting at me for not trusting them. I insisted on getting my swab tested from another outside laboratory also for being doubly sure. Before that I wanted to talk to my family members. I could not directly contact them since I was not supposed to keep my mobile phone. They did not allow me to talk to my family members on the pretext that the mobile phone or the landline phone would get infected. Another nurse came with the message that they have talked to my family members and they did not want any further tests outside. No second opinion is needed. It was very disturbing for me. Their strategy was simple. Once the patient is in, just hook him and keep increasing the hospital bill. I immediately sensed something fishy but had to keep patience to handle the situation properly. The night descended and after meals, I was allowed to walk in the corridor. While walking, I made friendship with a ward boy who was also residing in the same area as that of mine. He told the real story that was so startling.

With an alert look, he was whispering, "There is a big racket of selling the human organs going on, on the pretext of treating corona patients. The hospital belongs to a very influential personality of this region Mr Y K Powar who got government approval to open a hospital namely "Corona Corner" dedicated only to corona patients. The main objective was to run the racket of human organs illegal trading. Once a patient is admitted they make it sure that they are not discharged before serving their purpose. Seriously ill persons were treated and discharged after charging them hefty bills. Since they could not kill or use everybody for the human organ racket, they used to pick and choose. Patients with minor health problems and having basically healthy bodies were more targeted to provide a healthy organ. No patient is released easily on the pretext that the government did not allow them to be released. Even reports are manipulated. It is better if I run away from here. Sooner the better."

I felt like the ground slipping under my feet. Totally flabbergasted to the core, a kind of sparkling sensation ran through my body. For me it was the question of life or death. But before leaving, I had to make it sure that I should find some proof. The ward boy was ready to help. At midnight, I requested him to just sleep at my bed as my dummy. He handed me a mobile phone also. I slowly creeped into the store room and dressed myself with a full dress of Personal Protective Equipment (PPE). PPE is protective clothing, helmets, goggles, or other garments or equipment designed to protect the wearer's body from infection. Now I was looking exactly like a hospital staff, practically unrecognizable by anybody. First, I went to the operation theatre and found some activities going on. A patient came out with a bandage in the stomach. I was instructed to help take the stretcher to the observation room. To my great surprise, there were ten other patients in the same condition. I could not understand why operation is required on corona patients. Practically all of them were looking healthy. I took a snap of them and started recording the voice of a doctor nearby.

He was instructing a junior doctor, "Take care of these patients so that they should not get awake before four days. A Russian technology is to be employed during this period so that there will not be any scar of the incision of operation in their stomach and nobody outside should know that he was operated on. This is a secret work that has to be done perfectly and to keep it a secret you would be awarded suitably."

The junior doctor looked scared. But he was warned - if he did not cooperate, he would be jailed along with everybody. The Director's room was adjacent to the operation theatre. Some heated argument was going on there. I was overhearing the discussion very clearly through the wooden partition. One of them was telling whatever they were doing was not correct legally and was not ethical. In case the matter came out open in the media, all of them would be in trouble. The next stern reply was from someone authoritatively, maybe he was the Director, that the staff should just do as being told and they did not need to worry since the owner was a very powerful person and had lots of say in the present government. In case something happens, the authority will take all the responsibility.

I was just recording the whole discussion. According to him, patients would never know that their internal parts had been removed since they were brought to the operation theater under heavy doses of anesthesia. They were purposely kept under heavy sedative dose for 4 days after operation so that the incision cut is fully healed fast using the special Russian technology. Internally they would fully recover by the time they were discharged. The staff had to maintain utter secrecy. After all, they were being paid a practically double salary comparatively. Suddenly there was a sound of somebody entering the room. I kept myself hidden for some time till the person left the room and then I moved slowly outside. The proof was sufficient for me. I promptly sent all the proofs to my mobile number for future use. I went back to my ward directly to the change room. After changing my outfit, I was wearing again the uniform of a patient. Meanwhile the ward boy impersonating me so long was getting restless. He felt a sigh of relief the moment he got the sight of me. All other patients were fast asleep. I slowly creeped into my wrapper.

The next problem was how to get out of the hospital. It was sure that they would not allow me to go out so easily from the heavily fortified campus with a number of security personnel. Presence of some bouncers was making the exit further difficult. I knew that they preferred healthy persons and hence I might be one of their prime targets.

My next task was to do the reconnaissance. Every day at 1:30 pm there was change of duty time for security staff. Handover and takeover used to take 15-20 minutes. During this period the security was somewhat relaxed. I thought, this might be the right time to escape to the terrace since escaping through the main gate was impossible. Roof terrace usually was locked but it was kept open from 1-2 pm so that some of the staff could finish their tiffin box in open air. Interestingly, the terrace was open and empty from 1:30 to 2:00 pm every day. The top floor was a little more deserted than other floors during this period.

Our lunch was usually served at 11:30 am everyday so that within an hour they could wind up the utensils and get ready for handover/takeover. My ward was situated just below the top floor. Next day, on the pretext of post-lunch walking in the corridor, I slowly slipped to the top floor. As expected, the terrace was empty. Before anyone could see me, I was already there at the terrace swiftly. Then I closed the door. Oh my god! To my great dismay, there was no latch to bolt it from my side. I found a drainage pipeline which could be useful for me to get down. Fortunately, there were some overhang projections at every floor that could help me to take a rest while descending down.

How unfortunate! A security staff turned up just after taking over charge of the next shift. I got so scared. I was in a hospital patient uniform. Now he would catch me and hand me over to the hospital authorities. For me, it was a matter of life and death. One corner of the terrace was filled with rejected iron structures. Quickly I grabbed a rusted iron rod in my hand. I had never attacked or killed anybody in my life. But it was a matter of survival. My survival instinct empowered me. It was now or never. I was hiding on one side of the entry to the terrace with the rusted iron rod tightly clenched in my hand. The security personnel entered unaware of my presence. I attacked with the rod at his head. He started bleeding. I was shivering so severely having a look at the pool of blood. But before getting faint he was moaning feebly and that was heard by probably another hospital staff. He entered and ran after me. I ran towards the water tank metal staircase with a rod in my hand and climbed to the top of the water tank. This person also started climbing the staircase to overpower me and was trying to convince me to get down. I ran towards the dead end of the water tank surface. After that edge, it was a valley of death. My survival instinct was so strong at that time that I decided to fight. The man was also having an iron rod in his hand. The first thing I did was to hit his iron rod so hard that it was thrown away and he was then empty handed. The next action was my strike to his leg and the moment he bent down, I hit his head. Immediately he fainted. I waited for some time. Nobody else came up. Then slowly I took another iron rod and inserted into the two hooks of the door which practically closed it.

My worry was that the person at the top should not get consciousness. Otherwise, he could have alerted others. Again, I climbed up to the water tank and gave another blow to his head and pushed him down to the terrace. I could sense that he was dead. Meanwhile the first person's breath was still running but he was still unconscious due to profuse bleeding. The second person was wearing white shirt. His body structure was comparatively smaller than the first one with stout built. I dipped my fingers in his blood and wrote on his back "Hospital Organ Racket - Save Us Please". I allowed the blood to get dry. Somehow, I lifted him and threw from the top to the ground level. There was a big sound of thud and the crowd walking on the main road started assembling around him. The man I threw, fell flat and his white shirt with my writing was clearly visible to everybody. Within no time police arrived from the nearby police station around 100 meters away. From the top, I could sense that the police station in-charge immediately took the decision to raid the hospital since around 20 police personnel were marching towards the main gate of the hospital.

Meanwhile the hospital security staff also got alerted and before they could reach me, I had to escape through the pipeline. I started descending floor by floor all the four floors taking rest at each floor; but was standing at the overhang of the first floor to avoid unnecessary attention. Nobody would notice me due to commotion. I could have been easily noticed in the dirty hospital uniform which was soiled while sliding down. Therefore, I kept on standing on the first-floor projection. It was already 06:30 pm and was getting dark with the heavy overcast sky. I waited till 08:30 pm, then slowly came down. First thing was to throw away the shirt of the hospital dress. Just in dirty pajamas and grown beard, probably mistaken as a beggar by passersby, I was walking in the dark to my residence nearby. My father was taken aback to see my condition. I cautioned him to keep mum and keep it a secret. Very quietly I entered the outside servant's bathroom and asked my father to get my dress.

By the time I came out of the bathroom, my father had informed my family that I was fine and was discharged from the hospital as a normal person as if nothing had happened. He also informed them that I was taking a bath in the servant's bathroom as a precaution. Everybody believed but my father. The words had already spread like wildfire about the raid in hospital. The TV was full of news in this regard. Everybody was asking, "who threw that man down?" We were on a stroll after a sumptuous dinner. My father looked at me with a deep gaze and just asked me "You, did it?" I said, "yes" and everything was crystal clear to him.   It was difficult for the police to find out about the patients since many patients were absconding taking advantage of commotion. The best thing for me was that the records of patients were being deleted from the computer, the moment the hospital staff heard of the imminent police raid. Yes, the first man whom I left alive could have identified me. But I came to know later that even he succumbed to his injury, although I did not want him to. But I know that by killing the two, I had killed the whole series of killer instinct. Still, nobody could find out who killed the killers from the "Corona Corner."

The reader must be having lots of questions. Who am I? How and when was I admitted to the hospital? Who was the owner of the hospital? What were their activities? How could they run such a big racket under the nose of government machinery and more so, just stone throw away from the police station.

To know all these we need to travel to the flashback: How coronavirus started in India? What was happening during the mid and peak periods of the epidemic? What were the negative and positive impacts of Covid-19 on the life of common and privileged people? How did I get a direct encounter with this virus? How did the world know the details about an organized crime of human organ export run at such a large scale by the authorities of a well reputed hospital? Finally, how did I land up in the nexus of human organ racket and my lucky survival by murdering two staff members of the hospital, a mystery unsolved forever? Finally, how did the police find solid proof to indict the culprits?

Let us first start with the initial coronavirus period when it was introduced in India by some students arriving from the city of Wuhan, China.

Life during the advent of coronavirus

It all started in December 2019. This is the story of India's city of Pune. It is one of the best and beautiful cities of India. Situated on a plateau at the altitude of half kilometer above the mean sea level, this city is the most preferred one by the people who want to settle at a particular place to spend cool retired life. It is famous as a naturally air-conditioned city with uniform temperature throughout the year except April till mid-May. You have a cozy life with no extreme weather. The best part is the combination of ancient and modern cultures. The central part is an old city with so many old structures and shops with articles of vintage era available even today. This is surrounded by model multistorey skyscrapers. That is why it is rightly known as the cultural capital of Maharashtra state of India. Being the home of many famous institutions and universities, this place is also known as an educational hub. Some fondly call it Oxford of east. With 5-6 large industrial estates surrounding the city this place is also most sought after by jobseekers. The booming IT sector is one of the main attractions for the technological world and budding engineers. You get the advantage of both large and small cities.

The festivities of Christmas were just over, and the citizens were now gearing up to celebrate the new year with all fervor. I have a small family of 4 members: myself Ankit 27, my elder brother Manoj 30, father Shridhar 65, mother Vaidehi 62 and a servant Kapil 35. A sober natured Kapil was the solution to every problem in the house and a favorite for all. Everybody used to call him with his elongated name 'Kapeeel' with extra love. And he didn't mind. We have a bungalow in Kasturba Society in a middle-class residence area known as Vishrantwadi. Some thirty years back this place was so peaceful and now with the latest developments, this is now known as one of the main areas of Pune with all hustles and bustles.

Shridhar, my father, was an engineer in Ammunition Factory, Khadki, Pune which is 5 km away. He retired 6 years back and is enjoying the post retirement government pension. Vaidehi, my mother, retired as administrative officer in Research and Development Establishment Engineers, Kalas, Pune just 2 kilometers away. She too is enjoying the post-retirement pension. Manoj, my lovely brother, a Mechanical Engineer, is working in Tata Motors, Bhosari 7 km away. Myself Ankit, is a Functional Consultant in the famous IT company Wipro Limited, Hinjewadi 22 km away.

Everything was smooth sailing. Life was going as usual and everybody was enjoying his or her life. The family had planned to get Manoj married in June. Preparations were on. The festivities of Christmas were just over. Still, everybody was in the festive mood as the new year celebrations were on the anvil. On the Sunday afternoon of 29 December 2019, Manoj was sifting through the channels of TV and suddenly he sprung up from the sofa and exclaimed, "Oh my God! A new kind of virus has been reported from China by WHO (world health organization). The WHO China Country Office was informed by Chinese authorities of cases of pneumonia with unknown etiology (unknown cause) detected in Wuhan City, Hubei Province of China. That means the causal agent of the disease was not identified. The first human cases of the disease caused by the novel coronavirus causing COVID-19 was subsequently named SARS-CoV-2. It is proving to be fatal in some cases. There is no medicine and vaccine known to cure it." We all got alarmed and a bit scared.

First time we heard the name novel coronavirus or COVID-19 and my first reaction was, "So what? We are safe. Let the Chinese face it and solve the problem." Seldom did I know that in the coming days it would be affecting almost everybody in the world.

We were busy preparing for the new year celebration on 31 December, 2019 and the TV news was still sticking to the same news which was not important for us until now. Retrospective investigations by Chinese authorities had identified human cases with onset of symptoms in early December 2019.

For the first time the world had started taking it with some seriousness. Still the world community was hoping to contain it locally and a pandemic situation was not at all imagined. The first confirmed death was in Wuhan on 9 January 2020. The first death outside of China occurred on 1 February in the Philippines, and the first death outside Asia was in France on 14 February.

On 21 January, 2020, WHO came out with the first authoritative 'Situation Report' on https://www.who.int/ that elaborated the situation as below,

"WHO received further detailed information from the National Health Commission China that the outbreak is associated with exposures in one seafood market in Wuhan City. The Chinese authorities identified a new type of coronavirus, which was isolated on 7 January 2020. China shared the genetic sequence of the novel coronavirus for countries to use in developing specific diagnostic kits. The Ministry of Public Health, Thailand reported the first imported case of lab-confirmed novel coronavirus (2019-nCoV) from Wuhan, Hubei Province, China. The Ministry of Health, Labour and Welfare, Japan (MHLW) reported an imported case of laboratory-confirmed 2019-novel coronavirus (2019-nCoV) from Wuhan, Hubei Province, China. National IHR Focal Point (NFP) for the Republic of Korea reported the first case of novel coronavirus in the Republic of Korea. As of 20 January 2020, 282 confirmed cases of 2019-nCoV have been reported from four countries including China (278 cases), Thailand (2 cases), Japan (1 case) and the Republic of Korea (1 case). Cases in Thailand, Japan and Republic of Korea were exported from Wuhan City, China. Six deaths have been reported from Wuhan City."

The initial follow-up actions taken were as follows:

"In China, National authorities were conducting active case finding in all provinces; infrared thermometers have been installed in airports, railway stations, long-distance bus stations, and ferry terminals; the Huanan Seafood Wholesale Market in Wuhan city was closed. In Thailand, fever screening of travelers from all direct flights from Wuhan, China was carried out. In Japan, contact tracing and other epidemiological investigations were underway, by the local health authorities in Japan; quarantine and screening measures have been enhanced for travelers from Wuhan city at the point of entries. In the Republic of Korea, contact tracing and other epidemiological investigations were underway; surveillance for pneumonia cases in health facilities nationwide was strengthened; quarantine and screening measures were enhanced for travelers from Wuhan at the point of entries."

I must say that the rest of the world was still sleeping over this issue. The fire in the neighbor's house becomes a serious issue only when it spreads to our house. The only thing known was that Coronaviruses cause disease in a wide variety of animal species. SARS-CoV was transmitted from civet cats to humans in China in 2002 and MERS-CoV from dromedary camels to humans in Saudi

Arabia in 2012. Several known coronaviruses are circulating in animals that have not yet infected humans. A spillover event is when a virus that is circulating in an animal species is found to have been transmitted to humans. Based on current available information, coronaviruses may be transmitted from person to person either through droplets or contact. The virus transmitting animal, yet unidentified, is believed to be sold at the Huanan Seafood Wholesales Market in Wuhan. Investigation was still ongoing to identify this animal, the source of the outbreak.

Even the alert from WHO was also of mild nature since everybody was confused about the origin and implication of this virus. General attitude was that it is a local problem and we just need to avoid any travel to or from China. There were no restrictions on flights to and from China all over the world. The Indian government, although alert, was still in wait and watch mood. The 'India Situation Report" was published on 31 January 2020 on https://www.who.int/ which reported as follows:

"On 30 January 2020, a laboratory confirmed case of 2019-nCoV was reported in Kerala. The patient, a student returning from Wuhan, is currently in stable condition and cared for in hospital isolation. GoI (Government of India) has initiated inflight announcements and entry screening for symptoms of fever and cough for travelers coming from China at 21 airports of India. MoHFW (Ministry of Health and Family Welfare) issued a travel advisory advising Indians to avoid non-essential travel to China. National Institute of Virology, Pune, equipped with international standards of expertise and capacity, has been testing samples of nCoV. Advisory were issues as follows: • Frequent hand-washing, especially after direct contact with ill people or their environment. • People with symptoms of acute respiratory infection should practice cough etiquette (maintain distance, cover coughs and sneezes with disposable tissues or clothing, and wash hands). • Avoiding close contact with people suffering from acute respiratory infections. • Within healthcare facilities, enhance standard infection prevention and control practices in hospitals, especially in emergency departments."

Meanwhile I had already planned a few months back to visit Dubai with my brother as a tourist. Cheaper return air tickets (INR 33,568 for two persons) with SpiceJet Airways were booked on 15 December 2019 for the tour from 18 - 24 February 2020. I had purposely selected SpiceJet since they also have the facility to provide tourist e-visas through their partner DNATA - MARHABA SERVICES who offer their services at a reasonable rate without any extra charge. If you provide the valid documents such as scanned copies of passport, national ID or Aadhaar number, passport size photo and confirmed return ticket, you get a tourist visa even within 4 days. However, it is advisable to get the visa one month in advance to avoid any complication if they have any doubt about your credentials. It takes 15-20 days to provide and clarify the queries. We had to pay just INR 13,698 including travel insurance for two persons. Visa approval had arrived to us by 28 January 2020. The next question was whether OTB is required on our ticket by SpiceJet office? While purchasing the ticket online, they reflected a notification "OTB Required." We got confused. OTB means 'OK to board' which is required to be put on a seal of OTB by the airline office if the passport is ECR (emigration check required). OTB is not necessary if the passport is ECNR (emigration check not required). I looked at my passport. It had neither ECR or ECNR imprinted on it. Finally, I wrote to the passport office and they confirmed that absence of ECR seal means it is ECNR. That means the OTB seal was not required before boarding. This is the specific requirement in case of any Indian visiting UAE. In fact, ECNR is for those who visit UAE for employment. Reasonably good, Sea View Hotel (Mina Road, Bur Dubai, Dubai, United Arab Emirates) was booked on 16 January 2020 through makemytrip.com at discounted rate (INR 26,000 for 6 nights 7 days double occupancy). We chose this hotel since it had a bus stop just in front of it. It was well connected with bus station Al Ghubaiba just a kilometer away. Al Ghubaiba also has a metro station. You can comfortably walk or take the city bus to go to Al Ghubaiba any time. The city bus has good frequency. The famous metro-junction Al Fahidi was around one and half kilometer away. You can change the metro of different routes from here. Although I could not get, it is better if you get the hotel within half kilometer of Al Fahidi or Al Ghubaiba. This will save a lot of your time and energy. Al Ghubaiba is a wonderful area with its sea coast nearby and the water taxi to cross over to the Spice and Gold market area. After crossing the gold market area, you get metro station Al Ras. Just keep walking and enjoy the local old market and people. You get the real feel of the old city here. Another thing to remember is that you should be ready to walk at least 10 kilometer daily to get the real feel of Dubai.

Mind you, you cannot just ride the bus and pay for a ticket in the bus. You need to have a NOL card issued by Dubai Government

Roads and Transport Authority (RTA) available at any metro station or bus station. We will talk about NOL cards a little later. For this, the first day you have to go to the metro station or bus stand either walking or by taxi. The reason I am describing this is that a local currency called AED is worth 20 INR and you feel bad while paying for the taxi which is costly. Our objective was to have maximum fun with minimum expenditure. Another fact cannot be denied that you get the real feel of the city only when you travel with local transport. Taxis just take you swiftly from place to place without you knowing the local stops, market and more importantly, the people. As I had said earlier, we preferred the DNATA to get the visa. Another advantage was that they provided a free of cost NIYO card. This is a forex or foreign exchange card. I did extensive research on the other forex cards available in the market. I asked my bank too. But I found the exchange rate too costly since they were charging heavy commissions. After all the enquiries, I found NIYO Global Card was the best option. Let me explain the advantages in the next paragraphs.

In case of a normal forex card, you first have to purchase a card, then load the foreign currency on it. This, in most cases, is a physical process. There is a mark-up that you are charged. While abroad, you spend some part of the money loaded on the card. Upon return, you again need to go back to your bank to convert the remaining forex into rupees and will be charged a mark-up again. This double charging of mark-up can be a sizable chunk of money for most users. Even if you get a card completely online, documentation like submitting your passport, visa and tickets for travelling abroad, is required at the time of buying a card as well as at the time of reloading or unloading it.

In the case of NIYO global cards the scores of benefits I found were many. This is an INR card, which can be used globally, including in India. Your INR is automatically converted to other currencies when you use your card and it works in over 150 countries. It has zero markup charge. At the time of settlement, you will only be charged the VISA exchange rate prevalent on that day, which is normally low. The card is fully supported by a NIYO mobile banking app on your mobile phone, through which you get real-time transaction notifications, transaction summaries, balance inquiries, custom bank statements, safety features, an ATM locator, an up-to-date currency converter, the ability to transfer funds, and much more. The card is valid for 5 years. You can use your mobile application to lock and unlock your card at any time. Currently there are no joining fees for the card. This card works anywhere in the world where VISA cards are accepted. The card can be used to withdraw cash at all ATMs that accept VISA cards. NIYO does not impose any fees on ATM withdrawals. However, the bank that the ATM belongs to, might have their own fees associated with withdrawals. You can transfer funds from your NiYO account to any other bank account in India. To ensure that your payment amount is as close as possible to the actual price of your purchase, it is recommended transacting in the local currency in Dubai to avoid DCC (Dynamic Currency Conversion) charges.

With all my doubts cleared, I had gone for this forex card. I must tell you - this was a very wise decision due to its convenience and cost effectiveness. Everything was online with not even a single visit to the bank. Even the card was sent to me at my home by a personal messenger.

Normally, you need to foresee the problems you may face when you arrive in foreign country. One of them is that sim card of your mobile phone does not work there. You need to have either local sim or the Indian sim should have facility of international/ local calling valid in Dubai. Again, the question was: which one is cheaper and convenient? Nowadays you get a free sim card at Dubai Airport. At passport control, the Customs Officer will hand you back your passport including a package with a free Du Dubai sim card. This is a great thing for visitors. But only sim is free and it comes with only 20 MB data and 3 min calling time which is nothing. You need to recharge it for further use. Best place to get it recharged are the duty-free shops at the airport. Dubai has three network providers Du, Etisalat and Virgin Mobile. The comparative rates were as below:

Du prepaid sim card:
The free sim card provided at Dubai customs, is a Du sim card. You can also get a free Dubai sim card at any Du shop in the arrival halls. The prices for the data packages are as below,
55 AED ($15) = 500 MB + 20 minutes - valid for 7 days.
75 AED ($20) = 2 GB + 40 minutes - valid for 14 days.
110 AED ($30) = 3.5 GB + 50 minutes - valid for 14 days.
The data of the above sim cards is only valid within the UAE, the eligible talk time can be used to call any number in the world.

Etisalat sim card:

In Airport there is an Etisalat shop and they sell the following prepaid Dubai sim cards:

105 AED ($29) = 1 GB data only
105 AED ($29) = 700 MB data + 40 minutes + 40 SMS.

Data of the above Etisalat Dubai sim cards can only be used in the UAE, calling and texting credit to any number in the world. Both packages are only valid for 14 days.

Virgin Mobile prepaid sim card:
Virgin Mobile Dubai operates on the Du network and the sim cards are available in any duty-free shop at the airport. They offer much better value for money.

125 AED ($34) = 6 GB data + 50 minutes
130 AED ($36) = 6 GB data, Local 50 min, International 50 min
171 AED ($47) = 10 GB data + 50 minutes
263 AED ($72) = 20 GB data + 50 minutes
339 AED ($92) = 30 GB data + 50 minutes
The above packages are valid for 30 days only within the UAE

Considering that I was going to stay for 7 days, I found the best package of AED130 of Virgin Mobile which amounts to INR 2700. But I had to check my local Indian network providers also. My brother's mobile phone and that of mine had Jio sims. Jio had the following plan available for his users.

Jio India Global Pack:
INR1101: Unlimited validity
Mobile Data = INR0.02/10 KB
Call back to India = INR2/min
Outgoing Local call = INR2/min
Outgoing International = INR100/min
Incoming call = INR2/min
Outgoing SMS = INR2/SMS

Comparing all the options, the Jio Global plan was found to be the best one considering my requirement of short-term visit. This was most affordable and exactly suitable to my requirement. I got both my mobile phones recharged with this option.

With all the basic preparations ready, the next very important task was to prepare the day-to-day plan to visit. As I said earlier that my plan was to visit Dubai with minimum expenses and maximum entertainment and fun. Best way to visit any place is to use the local transport. That saves money and also you get the feeling of the place. That is why the plan was meticulously crafted in such a way that you could touch all the important places by using local transport and avoiding the use of taxis which are very costly. I must mention here that the possibility of hiring a travel agency was also not overlooked by me before finalizing my plan. Therefore, I contacted some of the travel agencies in Pune. I got quotations from 4 travel agencies exactly mentioning the tourist spots to be visited by me. As expected, the tour packages offered by the travel agencies are very costly. Main thing that I did not like was the restriction put by practically all of them regarding the tourist spots and time to be spent at each spot. Further, I was not sure what kind of hotels they would provide. Worst of all was a total lack of freedom. I agree that with a self-designed plan, you must be fit enough to walk a lot. You may get tired at the end of the day. But that is the cost we have to pay to be a real tourist and to have real fun.   Another hindsight is that we would be groping in the dark to find the places. This apprehension is minimized by using GPS and mostly behaving like a naive wanderer not shy in requesting help from anybody, anywhere, anytime. That means never hesitate to enquire about same place from three different persons; like a dumb one. That is the right way to become a foolish smart. Finally, after lots of interactions with travel agents, email enquiries and internet search, the plan was meticulously prepared as follows:

Day 1: 18 February 2020
Dubai local time is 1:30 hours behind India. Accordingly, the first task was to set the mobile phone to auto search for local time. I had an evening flight on SpiceJet and hence the plan for that day was to arrive, stay in the hotel and take rest. Important things were to withdraw local currency from the ATM at the airport using Niyo Global Card even before going for visa stamping on our passport. There were many foreign exchange shops at the airport but I was warned by my experienced friends that they are exorbitantly costly as compared to ATM withdrawal, if you have a forex card available with you. Next immediate important thing was to get a sim card at the airport. But I had already recharged our mobile with an affordable international Jio package, hence this would not be required. My existing sim card would work properly. Only action needed would be to put the mobile phone on Du Network with whom Jio already has collaboration.

Day 2: 19 February 2020

Smartest thing for a tourist with wanderer's lust like me was to purchase a NOL card. This is an Arabic word meaning 'fare'. NOL card is a smart card that enables you to pay for the use of various RTA (Roads and Transport Authority) transport modes in Dubai with a single tap. You can use your NOL card to travel on Dubai Metro, Buses, Tram and marine transport modes like Water Buses. You can also use the card to pay for RTA's Paid Parking. The NOL Card is an electronic ticketing card that was released for all modes of public transport in Dubai services, in August 2009. This Card system was developed by Hong Kong-based company Octopus Cards Limited. A NOL Card is a credit-card-sized stored-value contactless smartcard that can hold prepaid funds to pay for fares on buses and trains within one or more of four "zones". The credit must be added to the card before travel. Passengers "tap on" and "tap off" their card on electronic gates at the metro station or directly in buses when entering and leaving the transport system in order to validate it or deduct funds. The cards can be purchased from Metro Stations and Bus Terminus only. These prepaid Cards can be "topped-up" online or at ticket machines or at ticketing offices by credit, debit card or cash. The card is designed to reduce the number of transactions at ticket offices and the number of paper tickets. You cannot travel with any mode of transport without this card.

Now my problem was to find out which card would be the most suitable for me as a tourist. They provide 4 types of NOL cards namely Silver, Gold, Personal - Cards and Red Ticket. As per the website of RTA, only silver and gold cards are suitable for tourists. Silver is for normal class travel and the gold one is for gold class which is similar to first class in India. As suggested by many travel bloggers, a silver card is the best bet. The basic cost is AED25 which can be topped up as per requirement. Its validity is for five years and is applicable to all modes of transport for all zones inside Dubai. Pleasantly surprising is that RTA provides another wonderful facility i.e., a weekly pass for tourists which is damn cheap considering the flexibility. For silver card holders, you need to pay just an additional AED110 for 7 days. And you are entitled for unlimited travels on all modes of transport. Just hop in and hop out of Metros, Buses, Trams and Water Buses as many times, anytime, anywhere and in any zone for 7 days. This is a tremendous cost saving in local transport.

So, the first thing first, on day 2, would be to purchase the silver card @AED25 and weekly pass @AED110. Of course, the first day you have to walk or go by taxi to a nearby metro station or Bus station and thereafter you are free to move using your weekly pass. Once the weekly pass was purchased, the plan was to visit the Miracle Garden and the Butterfly Garden adjacent to it, during morning hours till afternoon. The entry tickets over the counter were AED55 per person. Evening starting at 4 pm was planned to visit Dinosaur Park, Ice Park and Garden Glow all in one campus having the combined ticket of AED110 per person. Estimated time to return to the hotel was 9 pm.

As regards the travel route on this day, it may be noted that Dubai metro has a green line and red line. The yellow line is for trams only. Take the red line metro, stop at Mall of the Emirates station. Then take RTA Bus No. 105 and it will directly take you to Dubai Miracle Garden in 15-20 minutes. Alternatively, Dubai RTA Bus operates a bus from Al Ghubaiba to Dubai Miracle Garden every 30 minutes and the journey takes 43 min. There is no direct metro or bus from Butterfly Garden to Garden Glow, hence taxi travel is needed which takes 25 minutes charging AED50.

Day 3: 20 February 2020
Day 3 was to be devoted fully to the famous Dubai mall and iconic Burj Khalifa both in the same vicinity. Since day 2 would be quite tiring and only one site is to be covered extensively, it is suggested to start the day 3 a bit late, say at 11:00 am after taking full rest. The plan was to visit Burj Khalifa 124th Floor (Non- Prime till 02:30 pm), Aquarium and Underwater Zoo 03:30 pm, Dinosaur Skeleton (Free) 05:00pm and Fountain Show 06:00-08:00pm. The easy way to get from Al Ghubaiba to Dubai Mall is by Metro which takes 10 min but you have to walk a lot around 850 meters from Dubai Mall Metro station. If you want to avoid so much walking and preserve energy, the best way is to catch line 29 bus that takes 40 min and drops you directly at the gate of Dubai mall. Advance booking for Burj Khalifa is must, hence it is advisable to get the time slot of around 12:30 pm booked online. For other items there is no time restriction. Tickets for certain timings are as follows: Prime hours 3:00 pm - 6:30 pm @AED210 and non-prime hours 8:30 am - 2:30 pm @AED135. Evening must be kept reserved for the waterfront of the mall to see the beautiful fountain show. They also provide combo tickets for Burj Khalifa and Aquarium together which is a little cheaper. The combined tickets can also be purchased online. While going back it is always advisable to go by bus available at the gate of the mall since walking all the way to the metro station is not a wise idea after the tiring day. In case it is necessary for you to catch the

metro, better catch the bus at the gate of the mall and get down at the metro station which is just a second stop.

Day 4: 21 February 2020
The fourth day was planned for a long-cherished Dolphin Show. It is situated in Dubai Creek Park. NOL cards are necessary for entry to this park. If you don't have it, an entry pass is available at the gate counter in AED25 per person. Anyways, we already had a plan to purchase a silver NOL card which was to be used for entry. The campus has Dolphin Show and Bird Show each for 1 hr. 30 minutes. They have certain timings hence it was better to get online tickets in advance for the timings of your choice. Normal tickets are AED 105 for the Dolphin Show but on Monday, Friday and Saturday they offer discounted tickets @AED75 for the 11:00 am show. The tickets for the Birds Show were AED50. Coincidentally 21 February was Friday and hence advance booking was needed to be done for the Dolphin show at 11:00 am and Bird Show at 12:15 pm. Next point to visit was Dubai Frame at nearby Zabeel Park.

As regards transport, at 10 minutes' walk from the hotel, there is bus stop Falcon Intersection 1 where the bus takes directly to the gate of creek park. The bus timing has to be checked in advance on the RTA website which provides real time bus availability. From Dubai Creek Park to Dubai Frame, Zabeel Park, taxi is preferable. This is not very far. There is no direct bus or metro connection.

Day 5: 22 February 2020
This was the day to enjoy the beautiful beach walk and sea cruise. Before the beach walk, it was planned in morning hours to visit the famous Atlantis Hotel situated at man-made artificial island i.e., well known as Palm Jumeirah. The Atlantis hotel also has The Lost Chambers Aquarium with the entry ticket AED115. Post lunch time was to be devoted to the beautiful Marina beach walk and then JBR beach walk, finally catching the Marina Dhow Cruise with Dinner in the evening. The pick-up spot was near the JBR beach. The Dhow Cruise normally charges AED110 per person.

The transport plan was a bit complicated. There is no direct connection from Al Ghubaiba to Atlantis, The Palm Hotel. However, you can catch the metro to DAMAC metro station, take the walk to Dubai Marina tram station, take the tram to Palm Jumeirah, take the walk to Palm Gateway station then take the Palm Monorail (return ticket AED30) to Atlantis Aqua-venture. It takes, all together, around

1 hour hence better to start a bit early from the hotel. While coming back use the same route to come to Dubai Marina Mall tram station for Marina Walk. The Marina walk also has Dubai Marina Mall for relaxing. JBR beach is on the next side of the creek. Good thing is that there is an RTA water taxi regularly running from Marina Mall to JBR beach. You can spend some time at the JBR beach and then catch the Marina Dhow Cruise nearby. Enjoy the dinner cruise and come back to the hotel by taxi (AED15) or nearby metro. But the metro station is a little far. You will have to walk for a minimum 15-20 minutes.

Day 6: 23 February 2020

This is the day to get friendship with the old Dubai which is well known as Deira Market Area with small lanes and old markets. The day can be comfortably started at 11:00 am. This area houses the famous Dubai Gold Souk (a souk mean market) and Spice Souk. Right in the spice market, in the small lane, lies a Heritage House of famous poet Al Oqaili for which entry and guide are free. If time permits, Women's Museum Bait al Banat can also be visited for which entry ticket is AED8 per person. These may not take much time hence advisable to spend some time at Al Ghubaiba water front. After returning back, the evening can be enjoyed with Dubai's specialty Evening Desert Safari with Dinner.

As regards transport, within 150 meters from Al Ghubaiba metro station is Bur Dubai Abra Dock. This is a beautiful waterfront with sitting arrangement. It is a boat docking place and locals/tourists hop on a convenient 1 AED shared 15 minutes small boat ride to the opposite bank of old Deira market. Boat services can be availed early morning to late night. After coming back to the hotel, the Desert Safari people pick you up at around 3:00 pm and drop at around 9:30 pm. The booking for Desert Safari could be done at the hotel counter one or two days in advance. They charge AED150 per person.

Day 7: 24 February 2020

This would be the last day of our tour and the return flight was at midnight and hence it was planned to relax comfortably till lunch and start the day at 2:00 pm. First visiting point was planned to be Sheikh Saeed Al Maktoum House, a historic building and residential quarters of the former ruler of Dubai. It is Just 10 minutes' walk from Al Ghubaiba metro station. Alternatively, the morning hours can be spent at Jumeirah Public Beach. The hotel provides a free shuttle from the hotel at 10:00 am and back at 02:00 pm (Book in advance earlier night at hotel counter). Afternoon 04:00 pm - 07:00 pm can be spent at the famous Global Village that needs lots of walking to see all the pavilions of different countries with a variety of cultures. Bus no. 104 starts from Al Ghubaiba Station and takes 20 minutes to reach Global Village. After coming back to the hotel at sharp 08:00 pm, start for the International Airport for departure. In case a bus is not available at Global Village for Al Ghubaiba, take a taxi to reach the hotel on time.

Thus ends our meticulous plan to visit Dubai.

As we can see above, the program covers all the important places of Dubai. Some small changes can be made depending upon the actual time spent on a particular site and stamina to walk. Total estimate was just AED7000 or INR140,000 for both, which was much cheaper than those of the travel agencies' quotations. This estimate includes air ticket, visa charges, hotel booking, travel insurance, local conveyance and entry tickets excluding food cost. All these were possible along with freedom of choosing sites, flexibility of timings and maximization of tourist points covered.

While devising a nearly perfect plan, the shadow of coronavirus was always creating the hiccups in our back of mind. Now that all the bookings were done cancellation could cost me a lot. However, the situation in the first week of February was not that alarming. I looked into the "Situation Report" of WHO to get the feel of the real situation.

The World Situation Report dated 10 February 2020 reported as follows:
"Globally there were 40,554 confirmed cases, China 40,235 confirmed (6484 severe, 909 deaths) and Outside of China 319 confirmed (24 countries, 1 death). Therefore, it was mainly China-centric and most of the cases reported outside, had travel history to China. WHO's immediate strategic objectives were to: limit human-to-human transmission including reducing secondary infections among close contacts and health care workers, preventing transmission amplification events, and preventing further international spread from China. This could be achieved through a combination of public health measures, such as rapid identification, diagnosis and management of the cases, identification and follow up of the contacts, infection prevention and control in health care

settings, implementation of health measures for travelers, awareness-raising in the population and risk communication."

The Situation Report for India dated 13 February 2020 was as follows:

"The Ministry of Health and Family Welfare (MoHFW) reported 3 cases of coronavirus disease in Kerala. They had a history of travel to China. These patients were in stable condition and were being closely monitored in hospital isolation. The Government of India (GoI) has issued travel advisories requesting the public to refrain from travel to China and that anyone with a travel history since 15 January 2020 from China will be quarantined on return. Further, e-Visa facility for Chinese passport holders has been suspended and existing visas (already issued) are no longer valid for any foreign national travelling from China to India. A total of 645 persons evacuated from Wuhan, have been quarantined at the camps maintained by Armed Forces and ITBP. They all have been tested negative. In Kerala, the situation has stabilized with no new cases being detected since the past one week. The State has lifted the state calamity status on 7 February in a high-level meeting chaired by the Chief Secretary. However, the state remains on guard and the surveillance strengthening, contact tracing, isolation and response activities are ongoing. The basic principles to reduce the general risk of transmission of acute respiratory infections include the following:
• Avoiding close contact with people suffering from acute respiratory infections.
• Frequent hand-washing, especially after direct contact with ill people or their environment.
• Avoiding unprotected contact with farm or wild animals.
• People with symptoms of acute respiratory infection should practice cough etiquette (maintain distance, cover coughs and sneezes with disposable tissues or clothing, and wash hands).
• Within health care facilities, enhance standard infection prevention and control practices in hospitals, especially in emergency departments.

WHO does not recommend any specific health measures for travelers. In case of symptoms suggestive of respiratory illness either during or after travel, travelers are encouraged to seek medical attention and share their travel history with their health care provider."

UAE had reported 7 cases out of which 6 had a history of travel to China. No death was reported there. There were no restrictions on international travels to and from UAE. There was no thermal checking at airports for UAE travelers. As stated above, the Kerala State had even lifted the state calamity status. Even the GoI had issued no warning. It was a situation of wait and watch. Therefore, the best way was to take calculated risk. And hence we decided that we would visit Dubai as a tourist as scheduled and would take necessary precautions.

Let us now see how the travel actually materialized. It was also interesting to observe whether the meticulously prepared plan was really executable. Of course, we had to modify our plan a little.

So as scheduled, we departed from Pune International airport on 18 February 2020 evening.

At the emigration check they just ask us whether we had any cough, cold or fever and they just allowed us to pass through security check-in. We arrived at Dubai International Airport at 10:00 pm local time meaning the Indian time of 11:30 pm. We were expecting the baggage claim near our arrival lounge in the airport. But to our surprise we were told to catch a metro train to reach the baggage claim area. The short train takes to the emigration check area in 10 minutes. On arrival, the first task was to withdraw local currency from an ATM inside the airport. We withdrew AED500 and had to pay the additional charge of AED26 as an ATM charge. This is the fee normally charged anywhere irrespective of the location of the ATM. This is the charge per withdrawal irrespective of the withdrawn amount. That means even for withdrawing AED100 you have to pay AED26 as an ATM charge. Hence it is advisable to withdraw higher value for once. We had estimated maximum AED450 against food and local travel in 7 days, hence withdrew AED500. After that we went for emigration check. There were two counters: one for visa-on-arrival and other for visa holders. We were directed to the latter one. Our passports were stamped and as expected, we got free local sim cards while the executive returned back our passports and visas. Anyways, the sim cards were not of our use since we already had our Indian sims with an international package in our mobile phones. To get the local network, we had to just search the Dubai network operator Du and our mobile phone started working locally.

It is always better to catch the government operated taxi service. The Dubai Taxi Corporation is a subsidiary of the Dubai Government Roads and Transport Authority (RTA). It operates official taxis in Dubai. All these official taxis have cream colored bodywork and red colored roof. Fares of these taxis are regulated with starting fare AED 5, then AED 1.82 per kilometer and waiting charge AED 0.5 per minute. Night charges are little more. Advance booking charge is AED 5 additional. This government taxi has a separate counter at the airport. Other taxis may charge you more.

We used this cream-colored taxi with a red roof to reach our hotel, we reached the hotel room at 12:30 am and we slept at 01:00 am which was 02:30 am as per Indian time. Next morning, we got up at 07:00 am but still half sleepy and did not feel like moving out. But the programs were already set up and we did not want to miss any site. This was the first fault we found in our itinerary. Considering the time difference between the two countries and for getting used to new places, we need to have sufficient time to get acclimatized locally. Ideally you should reach Dubai latest by afternoon and take full rest on the first day. Therefore, when we started out unwillingly, we were already feeling tired. As per our original schedule, we had to visit the miracle garden, butterfly garden and glow garden on this day. Before that we have to purchase the weekly pass along with a silver NOL card. We walked from our hotel up to Al Fahidi metro station in Dubai and purchased a silver NOL card with weekly pass @AED270 for both of us. As I had told you earlier, Dubai has two metro lines, green and red. We had to go to the Mall of Emirates metro station which is on the red line. But our starting point, Al Fahidi metro station, was on the green line and hence we had to change the train at BurJuman metro (junction) to get into the red line. After getting down at Mall of the Emirates station, we took RTA Bus No. 105 that directly took us to Dubai Miracle Garden in 15 minutes. Local transports in Dubai are very fast and punctual, hence it didn't take much time in reaching the desired destination. We were getting used to the new system and were very careful to tag in and tag out our NOL cards on departure and arrival. Metro stations have tagging machines at the entry and exit gates but buses have the machine inside the bus at the entry and exit gates. We had started getting the feel of the fun of the automatic systems of Dubai. The moment we entered the miracle garden after getting ticket AED55 each, we felt like arriving at heaven on the Earth. A beautiful arch of flowers greeted us and then it opened up a unique world of fantasy. Spread in 18 acres, the garden with well-maintained huge flower structures of different shapes and colors was just enchanting. Although it may be quite tiring, it is always better to visit this area on foot. You can take rest at some food stalls also. They have a facility of battery-operated vehicles at additional cost for the people who cannot walk. We stopped for some moment at umbrella garden to take snacks and cold drinks. It is claimed to be the world's largest natural garden. Their website claims:

"Every year from mid-November to mid-May, a 72,000 sqm space full of scents and colors comes to life. This incredible experience is one of Cityland's signature creations – Dubai Miracle Garden. It was launched on Valentine's Day, 2013, and is set in the heart of Dubailand. Seeing the garden in full bloom with its 150 million flowers arranged in colorful arches and patterns, and the myriad shapes they form, is truly magnificent. Dubai Miracle Garden's breathtaking landscaping has earned two Guinness World Records for the largest vertical garden in 2013 and world's largest floral sculpture forming the shape of an Airbus A380 in 2016. We received the accolade for the Tallest Topiary Sculpture on 25 Feb 2018. The 18-meter sculpture feature is Disney's first character floral display in the Middle East and is made from almost 100,000 plants and flowers, and weighs almost 35 tons."

While roaming around and bewitched by the surroundings, we forgot our tiredness.

Next destination was the nearby butterfly garden. After acquiring tickets AED55 each we first arrived at the main dome with lots of exhibits to purchase. It had a photo gallery of the founder of the garden and a butterfly museum. Butterfly Garden claimed to be the "World's Largest Covered Butterfly Garden" consists of ten custom-built domes around 6,673 sq. m. Each dome is filled with thousands of beautifully winged creatures, featuring 15,000 butterflies of around over 50 varieties in different sizes and colors fluttering around us. Dubai Butterfly Garden gives you the opportunity to see how butterflies evolve through each stage. Dubai Butterfly Garden has a climate-controlled dome, providing the butterflies a relaxed environment and permitting the domes to be open throughout the year. Along with the garden, there is also a butterfly museum and a lush green garden that is built with varieties of plants and flowers, fountains, birds and fish ponds.

We passed one by one through each of the domes devoted to different types of butterflies. The best part was playing with them. They were human friendly. How thrilling it is when a butterfly suddenly out of nowhere descends on your head or shoulder. You can take it on your finger and fondle it. We took lots of snaps with them. They were freely roaming around in each dome. For the first time I had seen the human friendly butterflies. It was like a childhood dream coming true.

The next visiting spot glow garden's timing was 4:00pm to 8:00 pm. It was around 20 km from the butterfly garden by taxi (AED50). But we were too exhausted to visit there hence decided to modify the schedule and go back to the hotel. The glow garden needs lots of walking and with already drained energy, who can dare visit it? That is the advantage when you are not dependent on travel agencies and their schedules. Anyway, on the way back to hotel, we stopped at Dubai Mall metro station and got advance booking for Burj Khalifa and Aquarium for the next day.

Day 3 was quite eventful. We had booked the ticket for Burj Khalifa for the time slot starting 11:00 am hence we started from the hotel accordingly. Although bus and metro trains both were available from Al Ghubaiba, we preferred metro since it is faster. As mentioned earlier, the iconic Burj Khalifa is situated in the vicinity of the famous Dubai mall hence we dropped down at Dubai Mall metro station. Although the mall is around a kilometer away from the metro station, it is directly connected through a long air bridge. We had to just keep on walking. But soon we realized that there was no point in walking a kilometer unnecessarily and wasting our energy since the bus number 29 was directly taking us from Al Ghubaiba to the gate of the mall. It is always advisable to save your energy for the travels in the day ahead. This was another mistake that you need to learn.

It was a long-cherished wish fulfilled when we climbed up to the 124th floor of Burj Khalifa within a minute through a very fast lift. It appeared as if we were right on the top of the world. All the multistory buildings nearby were dwarfed by its sheer height. The sea coast at some distance was adding to the beauty of the landscape. Beautifully designed waterfront of Burj Khalifa was looking magnificent from the top. We took unlimited snaps and spent around two hours in the food court and shopping area at the 125th floor. It has a total 160 floors but visitors are allowed up to 148th floor at some extra cost. Having lunch at this phenomenal height was itself something unique. It is supposed to be a flexible structure and hence has the margin of moving side by side by 3 meters to sustain the high wind speed. You literally feel the vibration caused by the swaying of the building side by side if you minutely observe. In general, while walking you may not feel the sway. We also found some important facts about this gigantic structure as follows:

"The Burj Khalifa height is a staggering 828 meters with 160 stories. It is three times as tall as the Eiffel Tower. It was designed to be the centerpiece of a large-scale, mixed-use development to include 30,000 homes, nine hotels, 3 hectares of parkland and the 12-hectare artificial Burj Khalifa Lake. It was constructed in 6 years. Besides having the world record for being the tallest building in the world, the Burj Khalifa is also the tallest freestanding structure in the world and has: -the highest number of stories in the world, -the highest occupied floor in the world, -the highest outdoor observation deck in the world, -the elevator with longest travel distance in the world and -the tallest service elevator in the world. The building has the longest single running elevator, which is 140 floors. The Burj Khalifa elevator speed is 10 meters per second, making the elevators among the fastest in the world. The Burj Khalifa elevator time to reach the observation deck on the 124th floor is only one minute. The tip of the sphere of the Burj Khalifa can be seen from up to 95 kilometers away."

Now, a few things to take into account when you plan to visit this structure. Generally, it is crowded and you may not get the ticket for immediate visit and hence better to get the ticket in advance. Even while having the ticket, you need to keep sufficient time margin for walking a lot to go up to the elevator section. At the elevator entry you will find a long waiting line. While descending down we found more crowd and waiting time.

After coming out from the Burj Khalifa we came to Dubai Mall which also has an ice-skating rink, gaming zone, and cinema complex, if you're looking for more entertainment options. But we directly moved to Aquarium and Underwater Zoo. I must say that this is one of the largest aquariums of the world with huge sea creatures under glass enclosure. The bewitching attractions were as follows:

"Dubai aquarium and underwater zoo has three main sections that offer unlimited marine exploration through unique experiences. Aquarium Tank is home to 140 species of thousands of interesting aquatic animals. This is amongst the largest suspended aquarium tanks in the world. This fascinating world is inhabited by sharks, rays and myriad other vibrant marine creatures that will make the kids squeal in delight. The tank also boasts of the largest collection of Sand Tiger sharks in the world. The Aquarium Tunnel is a 48-metre-long walk-through tunnel through which you reach the wonderful world of underwater-zoo. The Underwater Zoo, located on level two above the aquarium tank, allows you to discover the amazing range of aquatic animals through 40 different display tanks. Comprising three different ecosystems – Rainforest, Rocky Shore and Living Ocean, you encounter fascinating creatures like the Humboldt Penguin, Piranha, African Dwarf Crocodile, Giant Spider Crabs, Otters, Lionfish and so many more. The lovely part was the otter getting its heart beat checked by the veterinary doctor inside. We had the unsatiated luxury of photography. Finally, you get the experience of a lifetime when you meet the most powerful crocodile in the world weighing a whopping 750Kgs. You are awestruck by just getting the first sight of this majestic animal. The last and equally exciting is UAE's Night Creatures. This is another amazing and educational journey through the world of exotic and wonderful wildlife of the Arabian Desert housing Giant Camel Spiders, Arabian Toads, Fruit Bats, Veiled chameleons and many more. Wow! You get an ice cream parlor, the moment you come out. Not a bad choice to get yourself chilled after an exhaustive run through."

We got exhausted by these two sites hence were looking for a place to coolly sit and relax for some time before venturing to the next item of water front in the evening. One of the staff of the mall suggested Human Waterfalls inside the Dubai mall where the cascading water occupies the height of the mall. With its wonderful ambiance and entertaining aesthetic features, it is a favorite relaxing point for families. It is surrounded by palm trees to replicate the soothing atmosphere of a true desert oasis. With a diameter of thirty meters and a height of twenty-four meters, it has dazzling human sculptures with their hands spreading sideward, appearing to plunge downwards to the waterfalls. The rhythmic water flow is a visual treat. After relaxing for half an hour, we moved to the 155-million-year-old Dinosaur skeleton in Dubai Mall just before the entry to the waterfront area. Measuring over 7 meters high and 24 meters long, this humongous skeleton is a genuine fossil of a Diplodocus longus, a long-necked, whip-like tail sauropod that roamed the face of the earth millions of years ago. It is the most original skeleton finding of a Diplodocus longus in the world today, with over eighty percent authentic fossil bones. No tickets are required. I found the best part that the original and genuine information was provided in continuously running audio visual display screen. Brochures were also available for those interested in details.

By the time we completed the Dubai Dino visit, the sun had already gone down to the horizon and a dreamy dusk settled over the beautiful waterfront. It was the time for fun and relaxation after the hectic day. This place is famous for its Dubai fountain show. The skyrocketing and dancing fountain show under colorful lights in the backdrop of Burj Khalifa was a dream come true. We selected a particular site in the middle to settle on the staircase of an open court so that a panoramic view of the fountain show could be observed without any hindrance, suitable for photography. This thrilling attraction is the biggest choreographed fountain in the world, thanks to its ability to spray water up to 500 feet and its impressive length of 900 feet. Over 20 color projectors and 5,000 large state-of-the-art incandescent lights are used to illuminate the show which are choreographed wonderfully with a variety of musical tracks. No tickets are required. Just have fun. Enjoy snacks on the waterfront sitting on the cozy seats of a series of restaurants. Each fountain show is timed for around 15 minutes and repeated in every 20 minutes. The dreamy sequence culminated at 08:00 pm and our eyelids were drooping due to pleasant hangover. We took the wise decision to catch the bus for Al Ghubaiba right at the gate of the mall rather than travelling by metro. The bus took around 30 minutes to reach Al Ghubaiba. The satisfying day ended with us dropping into our cozy beds after hurriedly gobbling up dinner.

Day 4 was another exciting day with the first of its kind experience of dolphin show and bird show in the Dubai Creek Park. We had already taken the advance online tickets for both the shows. Being Friday, we got the discounted tickets. Previous day we were so tired that we got up the next morning at 9 am. By the time we got ready, it was 10:15 am and our Dolphin show ticket was at 11 o'clock. Although the bus was available, we could not have made it on time if we had preferred the bus travel. Therefore, we hired a taxi to reach the Dubai Creek Park. The entry to this park needs you to have an NOL card and that we already had. We had to hurriedly rush to the show to catch it on time. To our great surprise, there was a long queue and we needed to convert the soft copy of tickets to hard copy. Finally, we reached just on time in the hall where the Dolphin show was to be displayed. The Dolphin show was once in a lifetime experience. It is in fact a dolphin and seal show. Dubai Dolphinarium is home to bottlenose dolphins and Northern fur seals. These dolphins and seals were bought from Russia and even the trainers and demonstrators were Russian. Spread in a 5,000 square meter area, the modern marine facility has around 1250 seating capacity. The Dolphins have their living area with 600 cubic meters of sea water connected to the main arena pool. The dolphinarium complex also features kids' activities, birthday parties, school field trips, group events, trampoline, swim with dolphins, mirror maze, bird show, a restaurant providing snacks and a mini-5D cinema theater. A family of all age groups can easily spend 6 hours of fun time here. For us, the dolphin and seal show were more than enough. The amazing human-like acts of dolphins and seals were a hundred percent entertainment. Some of the enchanting acts were: high jump, long jump, playing ball, singing, jumping through a ring, water dance, clapping, swinging ring and saying bye-bye. At extra payment, you can have a close encounter with the dolphin and take a snap together. If you are a good swimmer, you can even enjoy swimming with dolphins. We had a next appointment with the famous Creek Park Bird Show immediately on the same campus. After an extraordinary dolphin and seal show, the bird show appeared a little lackluster. This is a typical human psychology. But I must confess that this was one of the best birds shows I have seen. At some extra cost, the visitors are also allowed to interact, take snaps and feed them. The interesting acts of the birds were: singing, dancing, cycling, fly past, talking and circus. We had a unique chance to see for the first time some of the exotic birds such as:

- Green-Winged Macaw: Also known as the red-and-green macaw, is the largest of the Ara genus, widespread in the forests and woodlands of northern and central South America.
- Blue & Gold Macaw: Also known as the blue-and-yellow macaw, is a large South American parrot with blue top parts and yellow under parts.
- Eclectus Parrot: The eclectus parrot is unusual in the parrot family for its marked visible light sexual dimorphism in the colors of the plumage.
- Cockatoo: A cockatoo is a parrot that is any of the 21 species belonging to the bird family Cacatuidae. Cockatoos are recognizable by the showy crests and curved bills.
- Double Yellow Head Amazon: Known as the yellow-headed amazon.

- Orange-Winged Amazon: Known as loro guaro, is a large amazon parrot. It is a resident breeding bird in tropical South America.
- African Grey Parrot: Is an Old-World parrot in the family Psittacidae. It is a medium-sized, predominantly grey, black-billed parrot and may live for 40–60 years.
- Indian Parakeet: Known as the ring-necked parakeet, is a gregarious tropical Afro-Asian parakeet species that has an extremely broad range.
- Red-Billed Toucans: The white-throated toucan is a near-passerine bird in the family Ramphastidae found in South America throughout the Amazon Basin.
- Silver-Cheeked Hornbill: A large species of hornbill found in Africa. It measures 30 inch in length, and has a very large cream-colored casque on the beak.
- Lanner Falcon: The lanner falcon is a medium-sized bird of prey that breeds in Africa, southeast Europe and just into Asia.
- Rock Kestrel: A bird of prey species belonging to the kestrel group of the falcon family Falconidae.
- Sun Conure: A medium-sized brightly colored parrot native to northeastern South America.
- Red-Billed Hornbill: A group of hornbills found in savanna and woodland of sub-Saharan Africa.

By the time we completed the shows, it was mid-day and we enjoyed lunch in the campus.

Let me remind you that we had skipped the famous Glow Garden on day 2 due to lack of time. But as per the schedule, we were supposed to first visit the Dubai Frame this afternoon. The famous Dubai frame is housed in Zabeel Park. To our pleasant surprise, somebody suggested that the Glow Garden is connected to Zabeel Park through a foot over bridge. We hired a taxi from Dubai Creek Park to Zabeel Park which was just 5 km away. UAE had Friday as a weekly holiday, hence thousands of families were gathered in the park on this day with their barbeque set-up and sport items. Dubai Frame, a gigantic 150-meter-high picture frame is one of Dubai's latest sights. The information obtained from some websites are as follows:

"The two towers of the Dubai Frame are connected by a bridge which is all of 100-square-metres, with a 25 sqm glass panel inset right in the middle of it. This glass walkway offers a fabulous 360-

degree view of the whole of Dubai. The Dubai Frame was designed by architect Fernando Donis. It stands tall at 152 meters and is 93 meters wide. The height of the Dubai Frame in regular terms is the height of a 50-storeyed building. The Dubai Frame consists of a Dubai Past Gallery, Dubai Future Gallery, Sky Deck, Social Media Wall and Souvenir Shop where you can buy tiny replicas of the Dubai Frame along with other souvenirs to take home to your loved ones. The Dubai Frame can take only 200 visitors per hour. Only groups of 20 will be sent to each of the augmented-reality stops – the Mezzanine level, the Skydeck level and the Vortex Level. Tickets must be purchased in advance according to the time slots based on batches."

After taking enumerable pictures, we walked over the footbridge connecting Zabeel Park and Glow Garden. We crossed over to Glow Garden by 5 pm which was the right time considering its opening timing of 04:00 pm to 11:00pm. Glow Garden, spread into 100 acres, has three attractions: Ice Park, Dino Park and Garden Glow. We got the tickets at the entry gate @AED110 per person. This is in fact the back entry gate. Main gate at the front is on the opposite side near Dino Park. From the back side entry, you first encounter the ice park, one of the 'coolest' spots in Dubai. To sustain the biting cold inside, they provide you first the warm jackets before entry. The 'Frozen Glowing Safari' theme, created skillfully by 150 talented artists from around the world, has been done with 5,000 tons of ice and is being maintained at a temperature of -7 to -8 degrees Celsius. Talented artists including many from Russia and China worked on beautiful sculptures that stand out in the park; they are made of ice, and carved to perfection. The artfully illuminated and elegantly crafted sculptures hold you in awe. The ice sculptures include more than 50 animal statues of Arabian horses, mountain gazelles, camels, falcons, lions, tigers, leopards, gorillas, pandas, giraffes, kangaroos, ostriches, peacocks and other creatures. It also features Abu Dhabi's Sheikh Zayed Mosque. For us, the cold inside was unbearable and hence we quickly completed the round and came out to our great relief. For the first time we realized how our soldiers are protecting our nation at subzero temperatures at northern borders under hostile weather.

The next item was Dino Park. This is probably the largest collection of models of Dinosaurs spread into about 20 hectares. It takes you to a prehistoric era when all these humongous creatures were roaming around on the earth millions of years ago. The models were mechanically moving with sound effect giving a natural feeling.

Each of them had information written in detail to make them very educational. It's the first of its kind Dinosaur Park in the Middle East. Started with 100 life-size animatronic dinosaurs, the park now has 120 of them. It's open only during winter months. The main idea behind this park is to offer an amazing and rare educational experience with the right balance of fun, entertainment, and thrill. You will find so many eateries on the way. We enjoyed the special Turkish ice cream of genuine taste with a much-desired brief rest.

By the time we completed the above two items, evening settled and suddenly the whole garden started glowing with lighting arrangements of huge sizes and shapes. Glow Park is famous for one of the largest theme parks with light shows around the globe. The Garden Glow spans in 40 acres, and there are 32 installations in total. The Park has been specially decorated with recycled fabric. More than 10,000 LEDs are being lit at once that will take you to a whole new world for sure. The blinking and wavy lighting seems to take you to a huge party site, appearing a magical show, leaving you totally awestruck and mesmerized. It is really a celebration of life with these multistory structures well-lit with a riot of colors. We did not feel like coming out from this dream world even at 08:30 pm. But the next day was waiting for us to enjoy another exciting event. Hence, we had to move back to the hotel by metro train available at Al Jafiliya station half a kilometer away.

Day 5 gave us the real feeling of frequent hop in and hop out, taking advantage of weekly free travel passes on all the modes of transport i.e., metro, tram, monorail and water taxi; due to the complicated route of the sites. First, we entrained at Al Ghubaiba metro station to reach the DAMAC metro station. After some walking we reached the Dubai Marina tram station. The tram took us to Palm Jumeirah tram station. Again, a long walk on footbridge led us to Palm Gateway station to catch a monorail to see the famous Atlantis hotel situated in the world's famous artificial island Palm Jumeirah. Our travel weekly pass would not work at monorail as this is a private line. Hence, we purchased a return ticket at AED30 each since we had to come back in 2 hours. One-way tickets are costlier than the return tickets. The monorail short journey was a unique experience since we could see the panoramic view of the man-made artificial island where the landfills have been done like the branches of palm trees. Each of the branches had posh bungalows. The end part of the main stem of the tree-like landscape was the Hotel Palm Atlantis with its own beautiful private beach. The look of this hotel from distance itself was grand and eye-catching, in the background of blue sea water. The Atlantis Aqua-venture station was the last station or terminus of the monorail. The Atlantis hotel also has The Lost Chambers Aquarium with the entry ticket AED115 and the world-famous water sport arena known as Atlantis Aqua-venture. You can spend the whole day with all the fun. Yes, it is a bit costly. Since we had already visited the world's largest aquarium at Dubai Mall, we did not want to repeat the same at Atlantis hotel and enjoying Aqua-venture water park was not in our plan, hence we returned back within 2 hours after spending some quality time at its beautiful beach and having a quick look at the shops in the hotel's mall. With the return ticket we came back to Dubai Marina Mall tram station using monorail and tram.

From Dubai Marina Mall tram station, the wonderful Marina Walk is just 5 minutes' walk. We need not get confused with the Marina Walk as a beach walk. It is in fact a promenade i.e., paved public walk, along the seafront. Truly a must-visit destination in the city, Dubai Marina Walk is one of favorites of tourists and locals equally. It's a seven-kilometer, tree-lined promenade that winds around the architectural marvel that is the man-made marina, bordering the emerald-hued waterway. This picturesque waterfront attraction is a sight to behold – with yachts bobbing up and down on the water and the bright city skyline reflecting in blue water. A beautiful creek surrounded both banks with latest designed skyscrapers each with its unique architecture. I found a crooked design of twisted structure as a unique experiment by the architect. With a never-ending stretch of restaurants lining the edge of the waterfront, Dubai Marina Walk is really a lifestyle destination, thanks to the huge range of leisure, dining and shopping options. Midway to the walking length is the Dubai Marina Mall that houses well-known high street fashion brands, beauty brands, electronics and home décor stores. There is a kids' play area on the promenade, complete with slides, swings and climbing frames. The play area is lined with benches for mums and dads to relax. At the BYKY stands you can simply register at the stands and rent the bikes using your mobile phone number.

After walking half way through, we decided to take advantage of the close proximity of JBR Beach walk on the opposite side bank. Fortunately, there was a government run water taxi ready to cross us over to the other side in 5 minutes from the water station at Dubai Marina Mall. The famous JBR Beach area was just 10 minutes' walk from the bank on the opposite side. Jumeirah Beach Residence (also known as JBR) has a 1.7 kilometers long beach side walking trail. It is a residential area, located against the Persian Gulf in Dubai and contains 40 towers (35 are residential and 5 are hotels). The development, comprising four distinct plazas, occupies the bulk of the beachfront and seventy retail and food and beverage outlets, alongside entertainment facilities. Unlike Marina walk this was an entertainment at actual beach with vast sandy expanse and hordes of bikini clad western and local swimmers enjoying the cool water with sun bath. We preferred to enjoy the cool sea breeze sitting on the sand rather than walking alongside the beach. Sometimes just sitting and watching people's activity at the beach is also fun.

Our night had an appointment with the lovely Marina Dhow Cruise with Dinner. The pick-up place for the dhow cruise namely Al Wasal was at 1 km of walking distance. Dhows are typically trading vessels primarily used to carry heavy items, such as fruit, fresh water, or other heavy merchandise, along the coasts of Eastern Arabia. We had already booked the cruise in advance @AED120 per person. The rate is AED150 per person if you want pick-up from and drop-off at the hotel. It was a double decker ship beautifully decorated with LED lightings. We were lucky to get the window seats. As the ship was cruising ahead, the magnificently lighted Dubai skyline on both sides was giving the feeling of a dream city. Meanwhile a sumptuous dinner was served with cold drinks. A lively program of Arabian dance added to the flavor to the cruise. Unsatiating camera snaps with ever changing angles were the rich collection of memories. "Oh, this night should never end", was the voice coming from within. The unforgettable event ended at 10:30 pm. Now it was for us a tense moment. The tour organizer told us that metro trains service stops at 11:00 pm. We immediately rushed to the nearby Jumeirah Lake Towers metro station. On reaching the station with about 15 minutes' walk, it was a great relief to know that the last train was in fact at 11:30 pm. Probably 11:00 pm is the time for the last train from the starting station. We reached the hotel at 12:30 pm tired, but excited and exhilarated. What an eventful day!

Day 6 was purposely planned for half leisure-day since we slept very late last night. We started at 11:00 am comfortably. Just a few meters away from the Al Ghubaiba bus station, is the beautiful waterfront called Bur Dubai Abra Dock. It is a nice waterfront with seating arrangements and many snack centers. It is basically a boat docking place. You can find bigger boats or mini ships to take you to as far as Sharjah. Interestingly, there are many small boats regularly running popularly known as AED1 boats that take you to the opposite bank. On the way to the boat, you will find some nice small eating places right touching the water shore: a place to relax, eat and enjoy the ripples of water, laden with cool sea breeze.

On crossing the creek, we found the famous old Dubai city christened as Deira Market Area with small lanes and old market. This is called the old souk area (locally souk means market). Each lane is devoted to a certain category for the ease of clients such as Gold Souk, Spices Souk, Garments Souk, Perfume Souk, etc. We visited Gold Souk which had mind boggling varieties, designs and price ranges. Hundreds of gold shops in one campus with ornaments glittering under lighting was a great show indicating how crazy are the people in this part for gold. Then we moved to the Spice Souk after crossing the Perfume Souk. The display of unbelievable and colorful varieties of spices was the scene I had never seen before. We got some dates packed which is the specialty of this part of the world. But you need to bargain since they keep the price jacked up specially for tourists. Just in the midway of Spice Souk a small lane goes to the museum of one of the greatest poets of UAE, Al Oqaili. We experienced the atmosphere of one of the most beautiful traditional heritage houses made of coral, stone, plaster, chandal wood, teakwood, fronds and trunks of palm trees. The house consists of two floors, in which the rooms are distributed around an internal courtyard: a breathing space for the building. As long as you are there, it takes you to the ancient era of Dubai enlivened by a valuable set of collections, personal tools belonging to the poet, furniture and household items and his poetry collection in his handwriting. I loved the design of the balcony with wooden railing. The well-maintained museum was a great reprieve; a soothing change from sky-scraper modern Dubai. Lack of interest from my brother compelled me to skip the nearby Women's Museum Bait al Banat; as he was bored with overdose of history and downtown feelings even as I was enjoying every bit of them.

Sufficient leisure time at hand, allowed us to stroll around the cool waterfront in Al Ghubaiba. After lunch, we were back in the hotel by 02:00 pm since we had an appointment with a Desert Safari tour agency with pick time at 03:00 pm. He arrived right on time to pick us up.

A highway drive of around 70 minutes led us to the desert safari camp outside Dubai city; around an hour before sunset. The first item was called Dune-Bash, meaning an extremely rough ride through the uneven landscape of dune. The explanation of dune bash is beyond words. You have to experience it to understand it. They use a Four-Wheel drive (4x4) vehicle with a powerful engine which does not get stuck in sand. We were warned in advance to use the seat belts. There were a total 7 persons in the vehicle including 4 tourists from Malawi, East Africa. Within no time, the vehicle rushed at high speed to the nearby sand dune hilltop. Next moment it started descending down with the same speed leading us to the topsy-turvy route shaking all of us to our core. The African friends were literally wailing, out of scare. All of us were praying for the safety of our lives. The 20 minutes ride with a splash of sand scattering both sides was appearing as an unending journey. We had a sigh of relief when the show ended. Our enthusiastic driver was asking "Once more?". We said "No more!". Honestly, to the core of our hearts, we enjoyed the scary adventure although life was appearing at the end of cliffhanger. The Sun was about to set. And deep in the heart of the Red Desert, from the crest of high dune we watched the mesmerizing sunset with its orange glow over the vast expanse of rippling sands all around. A compulsive photography of an aeroplane passing through in the background of the setting Sun was unavoidable. Then there was a free camel ride for 15 minutes. We also got ourselves photographed in typical Arabian dress.

Now it was the time to relax in the Desert Camp on comfortable low cushions savoring sips of the delicious Arabian brew – Coffee and Dates. We had our hands painted with Henna designs. Finally, we enjoyed the delicious Buffet Dinner with a traditional barbeque. Adding to the flavor were Live Entertainment Shows – Belly Dance, Tanoura Dance, Fire Show, Arabian music. We also got ourselves photographed with a large eagle sitting on our hands and heads. The organizers dropped us at our hotel at 09:30 pm. The hangover of the unique experience was not ready to depart till we started dozing.

Oh no! The last and 7th day of our journey had arrived. We had the whole day with us since our return flight was at midnight. Every morning, a hotel staff used to insert a newspaper into our room. The local newspaper that day had big headlines "13 cases of coronavirus were detected in UAE with 6 having travel history to China. I exclaimed, "My God, we had completely forgotten corona." Although we always had the precautionary items such as sanitizer, soap, mask, gloves, etc., it never occurred to us to use them since there was no seriousness about this anywhere. In the public arena, the awareness had just started. Bus drivers were always wearing masks. One or two travelers in the metro, only with a Chinese (or Mongolian) look, were wearing masks. An advisory was issued to wash hands with soap, avoid crowds, use sanitizers, eat only hot meals, etc. and these, we were already following. There was no advisory for social distancing. It was like a confused cautious approach everywhere. If you recall, we had started the journey with calculated risk. For the first time, a spark of worry creeped in. But we were happy that all went well till now. The only time in the last 5 days we were worried was when we travelled through metro train in rush hours while returning back on the second day. Rush hours start at 5 pm and we realized that we should have avoided it: a third mistake in our journey. Buses are mostly not crowded and hence need to be preferred.

An important item on the 7th day was Global Village. We enquired about it with the hotel staff. She informed me that it starts at 4 pm and is always over crowded. Morning hours were to be spent with Sheikh Saeed Al Maktoum House, a historic building and former residential quarters of the former ruler of Dubai which is 10 minutes' walk from Al Ghubaiba metro station. Meanwhile we came to know that the hotel had free shuttle service to Jumeirah public beach 10:00 am to 02:00 pm every day. Hence, we decided to avoid the overcrowded Global Village due to coronavirus scare. We were safe till that time and did not want to take any further risk. Therefore, the best option was to visit the Jumeirah public beach. We enjoyed the beach to the maximum. Considering our presumably tiresome late-night return-journey to home, we took full rest in the afternoon with a mood of eat, drink, sleep and TV show. With an objective of reaching the airport 3 hours in advance we reached at around 08:30 pm. After completing the smooth procedures, our flight took-off on time at midnight and reached Pune at 05:00 am local time. A successful, enjoyable and more importantly safe tour ended with great satisfaction.

The story of my lovely Dubai visit will not be complete without some concluding remarks. Purchasing a weekly travel pass was a very wise decision. Arriving at Dubai by late night flight is not a good idea. We need to reach maximum by afternoon, take a rest on the first day and start sightseeing the next day. Sometimes we used to get too exhausted. One more day could have made our lives easier. We had estimated the total expenditure of INR140,000. We actually spent only INR130,000 which is AED6,500 or USD1,800. This is 25-30% cheaper as compared to most of the quotations received from travel agencies before starting the journey. All aspects have pros and cons in our life. Self-guided tour had freedom of time, choice of sites and cost effectiveness, but was tiresome. The guided tour of travel agencies could have been less tiring but with less -exposure, -fun and -freedom. So, the lesson for those who cannot walk a lot, is to hire a travel agency but with your plan and condition of time and site flexibility to some extent. It may be costly but comfortable.

When we returned back to Pune, there was a considerable extent of buzz about coronavirus in the country. A great extent of churning was going on in the government machinery to tackle any undesirable event. Everybody was sensing the advent of the pandemic but were not clear about the course of action. There were rumors of some drastic, strict and systematic actions to be taken by the local governments. SOP (Standard operating procedure) to tackle coronavirus in foreign countries were being studied. Especially, the case of the uncontrollable spread of pandemic in Italy was being studied in depth. The concept of "lockdown" in China was for the first time heard and was closely being watched by all the countries. The Indian nation and the society were mentally getting ready to face the inevitable. We felt a great sigh of relief to arrive back from UAE just in time, amid the stories of travelers getting stuck at certain places for days in some countries for mandatory quarantining. All's well that ends well.

The mid period of coronavirus

It took 3-4 days to recover from the hangover of the fantastic Dubai tour in the last week of February. By 1 March 2020, the news started pouring in from all corners that the Government of India is negligent while handling coronavirus. India must take stringent actions to avoid spread of the dreaded disease. Even in our case, no thermal screening was done when we arrived from Dubai. Naturally the government was a little skeptical that the country's economic activities should not stop and at the same time a focused effort to contain the disease in a localized way needed to be done. At that time, the main focus was to stop the import of coronavirus from other countries and hence thermal screening plus quarantining the affected passengers were the key steps. Following are the precautionary actions taken by the government before and after our arrival back in Pune:

17 Jan: The Ministry of Health and Family Welfare (MoHFW) announced thermal screening for all passengers coming from China (and Hong Kong) at Delhi, Mumbai and Kolkata airports.

21 Jan: Thermal screening of passengers coming from China expanded to seven airports: Delhi, Mumbai, Kolkata, Chennai, Bengaluru, Hyderabad and Cochin.

28 Jan: MoHFW stated in a release about the procurement of more thermal scanners for faster testing. Also announced screening at all major ports. Health Minister Harsh Vardhan stated that around 35,000 passengers had been screened already, as plans to implement such screening methods were underway for 20 more airports.

13 Feb: MoHFW announced universal screening for all passengers coming from Japan and South Korea, besides China, Hong Kong, Singapore and Thailand. Vardhan claimed that a total of 2,51,447 passengers had been screened from 2325 flights.

02 March: The Directorate General of Civil Aviation (DGCA) announced that the universal screening protocol has been expanded to all passengers arriving from Italy and Iran, besides China, Hong Kong, Singapore, Japan, South Korea, Nepal, Thailand, Vietnam and Malaysia.

04 March: MoHFW announced mandatory universal thermal screening at all airports and seaports, while requiring every passenger to declare their recent travel history.

11 March: Government of India suspends most visas/e-visas (except for visas related business, diplomatic work, UN/International organizations, employment and projects) from March 13, 2020 till April 15, 2020.

It is clear that UAE was not on radar till 4 March. We were lucky to escape the mandatory quarantine procedure marginally. On 19 March, Indian Prime Minister Narendra Modi in his nationwide broadcast appealed to citizens to observe a self-imposed "public curfew" on Sunday 22 March (07:00 am - 09:00 pm), "All citizens should abide by this and remain indoors, not visit any public places. For the past two months, millions are working day and night in hospitals and airports and those serving others without taking care of themselves. On March 22, at 5 p.m., we should stand on our doorways, balconies, in our windows and keep clapping hands and ringing the bells for five minutes to salute and encourage them."

The address was an attempt to curb an atmosphere of fear about the coronavirus outbreak that has affected 173 people, including four deaths in India. For the first time everybody in the country felt that there was something very serious. The Economic Times, India reported on 22 March with a heading "India observes Janata curfew, millions stay indoors". Details were as follows:

"As the 14-hour 'Janata curfew' got underway at 7 am, people kept themselves indoors as part of the social distancing exercise to help stop the spread of the virus. All markets and establishments except those dealing in essential goods and services are closed for the day………In the national capital, roads were deserted with barely some private vehicles and buses plying. Vendors were off the roads in the morning hours with people confining themselves to their homes………Commercial capital Mumbai observed the restrictions on Sunday with the usually bustling western and eastern express highways and other arterial roads wearing an empty look and people staying indoors to support the curfew………Traders' body Confederation of All India Traders (CAIT) had announced that they will keep their establishments shut across the country for the 'Janata curfew'."

As regards showing solidarity with health and services workers, The Hindu, 22 March reported, "Later in the evening, thousands of people expressed their solidarity with doctors, police personnel, health workers, sanitary workers and others, by coming out onto the balconies of flats in apartment complexes, rooftops and front yards, as the clock struck 5, on Sunday and clapped in unison. The family members, including senior citizens and children, came out and clapped, and some even took plates and other utensils to ring the bell."

In Pune too, it was a wonderful scene when all of us were clapping and used utensils to ring the bell for 5 minutes at 05:00 pm. The whole surrounding was in unison for salutation to front line workers with reverberating sound permeating all over. This was a great display of our resolve to face the inevitable lockdown in the near future preparing us mentally to face tough times for the sake of wellbeing for all. The appeal of the Prime Minister had worked like magic. This was the preparation to win a future psychological war.

The sequence of events was indicating that the government might announce complete lockdown anytime and as expected, Prime Minister Narendra Modi addressed the country at 8 pm on Tuesday, 24 March declaring a nationwide lockdown for 3 weeks from midnight. He acknowledged that 3 weeks is a long time and there would be a lot of inconveniences, but that these steps were necessary to prevent suffering in the long term. Given that there was no treatment, social distancing was the best possible defense. The PM urged to follow only doctor's prescriptions as self-medication can have harmful side effects. All government and private offices would remain closed, with the exception of those involved in essential services.

Later the lockdown was extended phase-wise as the situation was not improving. Following were the 4 lockdown phases:

Lockdown 1.0: 25 March 2020 – 14 April 2020 (21 days)
Lockdown 2.0: 15 April 2020 – 3 May 2020 (19 days)
Lockdown 3.0: 4 May 2020 – 17 May 2020 (14 days)
Lockdown 4.0: 18 May 2020 – 31 May 2020 (14 days)

Major restrictions implemented were as follows:

- Ban on people from stepping out of their homes
- All services and shops closed except pharmacies, hospitals, banks, grocery shops and other essential services
- Closure of commercial and private establishments (only work-from-home allowed)
- Suspension of all educational, training, research institutions
- Closure of all places of worship
- All transport services–road, air and rail, with exceptions for - transportation of essential goods, fire, police and emergency services, were stopped
- Prohibition of all social, political, sports, entertainment, academic, cultural, religious activities
- Services such as food shops, banks and ATMs, petrol pumps, other essentials and their manufacturing were exempted.
- The Home Ministry stated that anyone who failed to follow the restrictions could face up to a year in jail.

Then started the unlock periods. On 30 May, it was announced that lockdown restrictions were to be lifted from then onwards, while the ongoing lockdown would be further extended till 30 June for only the containment zones. Modi later clarified that the lockdown phase in the country was over and that 'unlock' had already begun. Restrictions were eased stage-wise in following steps:

Unlock 1.0: 1 June 2020 – 30 June 2020 (30 days)
Unlock 2.0: 1 July 2020 – 31 July 2020 (31 days)
Unlock 3.0: 1 August 2020 – 31 August 2020 (31 days)
Unlock 4.0: 1 September 2020 - 30 September 2020 (30 days)

All these were happening not without adverse social and financial impact. Raw food items were around 20-30% costly even with warnings from the government to traders against hoarding. Thousands of laborers emigrated out of major Indian cities, as they became jobless after the lockdown. Use of alcohol was reduced drastically resulting in loss of large revenues to states. India's electricity demand fell down considerably. As expected, the worst hit was the financial sector. The GDP growth rate had fallen from 8.2% in January-March 2018 to 3.1% in January-March 2020. In the first quarter of the financial year 2020-2021, this number went into negative. The GDP growth rate for April-June 2020 was -23.9%, which happened to be the worst ever in history.

Well, some good things also happened side by side. Supply chain of drug peddling was completely broken. Rivers had become cleaner as industries were closed due to the lockdown. The quality of air had significantly improved during the lockdown. Death due to road accidents reduced. Lots of money was saved with the standstill outdoor activities such as outside eating, tourism, fun trips etc. The most interesting observation was that people stopped getting sick due to extra precautions at home. Scare of getting contracted with coronavirus in hospitals, compelled the postponement of treatment for minor health problems. Those who were prone to visit doctors even for minor problems, were now boasting to be healthy persons. The doubling-rate of corona cases were getting delayed due to lockdown. A group of researchers at the University of Oxford who tracked the governmental policy measures to counter the pandemic, rated India's lockdown as one of the most stringent in the world, scoring "100 out of 100" on their tracker. They noted that India implemented school closures, border closure, travel bans etc.

Hundreds of thousands of laborers from all over the country had migrated to metro cities in pursuit of greener pastures. Most of them worked as daily wage workers or had temporary jobs. They lived in rented houses with minimum bare facilities. Majority of them led a virtual bachelor life leaving the rest of the family members at native places who took up farming activities. Every month, they sent the savings to their family members for better subsistence. With hardly any bank balance, they lived at the cliff of survival.

The saddest thing was the plight of the migrant labor force. The unprecedented lockdown had enforced complete closure of industrial, commercial and social activities. More than corona scare, the fear of unemployment was looming larger. Even the government has not foreseen the intricacies and consequences in context with migrant laborer. In absence of any guideline and policy for them, they found themselves in total disarray. The first reaction of typical human survival instinct was - escape. A dominant emotional thought was overpowering them, "What if the tragedy strikes me as I am far away from my nears and dears?" Therefore, the second instinct was to be with their own people as soon as possible. Living alive was more important than living with comfort. But all modes of transportation were discontinued. As a result, thousands of migrant laborers started on foot to their native places without caring for social distancing. The government machineries were caught unalarmed. It was a daunting task to control the mass exodus. Immediately the local governments announced that the labor force need not move anywhere and they would be provided with food and shelter. But how long? While government schemes ensured that the poor would get additional rations due to the lockdown, the distribution system failed to be effective. With factories and workplaces shut down, millions of migrant workers had to deal with the loss of income, food shortages and uncertainty about their future. Following this, many of them and their families went hungry.

On 1 May, the central government allowed the Indian Railways to launch special trains for the migrant workers and others stranded. But it was a slow process and could not have accommodated all. Many of them did not wait their turn to board the government-arranged transport, mainly due to starvation and eagerness to reach their homes soon. Additionally, they felt that going back to their hometowns, they could return to farming and take up small jobs. The mass exodus on foot continued albeit to a lesser extent with poorly managed crowds facing occasional starving, dehydration and sleep trauma. Local governments, NGOs and certain individuals were trying to help them to the extent possible. Nobody was prepared for such an unprecedented situation. Finally, the matter settled in a month. Whatever may be, but soon the commercial and industrial establishments started feeling the pinch of labor shortage. For the first time in the history of India, the importance of laborer was felt so strongly everywhere as the labor force was taken granted till now. Even with the government announcing the unlock phases, the economic activities got a bitter battering. Shortage of the labor force was one of the major causes for GDP growth rate going into negative figure.

Crippling effect on business due to absence of laborers, was never felt so hard. Until now unorganized service sector was one of the neglected and unregulated areas. For the first time many innovative ideas started pouring in. Some state governments were proposing that enough opportunities should be generated for the migrant labors at the native places. Industries and commercial establishments started realizing that the labor force must be given due respect and importance. Laborers working on critical sections were given the air tickets for coming back to work. They were wooing them with additional facilities for comfortable subsistence. Politicians were proposing to enact a new law for migrant laborer. Many laborers had taken a decision to stay back at their native places and continue with the farming activities with whatever income they had. All these changes were the matter of research for psychoanalysts and sociologists since the whole activities were resulting in a different kind of socio-economic change. Survival was more important than improving the standard of living. Some migrant laborers started returning back to work only after unlock 4.0, but by that time damage had already been done. The economic development had got a severe beating.

Life at the peak of coronavirus

The pandemic had snatched our normal life. It was frustrating to lead a life in forced seclusion. A gloomy atmosphere was affecting the life of everybody in all age groups and all sectors of society.

My next-door neighbor was Mr. Sudhir Sawant, a Chartered Accountant in a reputed company. His family was very close and friendly to us. They had a little boy Rajan aged 10. Since his toddler days, regularly intermingling with us, he was like our family member and never thought of us as a different one from his. Normally we used to play cricket in the lane. To his great dismay, he was forbidden to enter our house. Parents had restricted him in his house. I could see his sad face hanging his legs through the railings of his balcony every day and looking in oblivion. Even his school was closed and online classes were totally charmless for him with no friends, teachers and playground around. The lack of the freedom of open-air activities was creating an annoying feeling bubbling out as a chaotic behavior. His parents were complaining of his ever-increasing irritation resulting in a slow transformation of the obedient and cheerful boy to an unruly bastard. Day by day it was difficult for the parents to handle him. Children are a flowing pious river. How long can you stop them without repercussions of a cracking of an overloaded dam? All the options of opening sluice gates had been exhausted. Very few child psychologists had an answer to this unprecedented situation.

Chartered accountant is such a post that no company can do without him. That was the best thing to happen to Mr. Sawant so that his job was secured even in such a financial crisis situation. After the first lockdown period, he had to visit his office for day-to-day work, but by following a standard operating procedure (SOP). Seriousness of the situation can be assessed with the details of SOP as given below:

- Ensure proper hygiene at the workplace including washrooms, water containers etc. Disinfection and sanitization of all common areas by properly PPE equipped staff.
- All the employees will be provided with masks and gloves. Avoid use of AC to the extent possible and use natural ventilation by keeping doors and windows open.

- The resuming of employees at workplace will be done in phases with timelines and dates, presence of employees at workplace in a day should not be more than 33% of total strength.
- Each employee self-declaring their health status as per the prescribed proforma
- Those requiring monitoring will be referred for medical advice before resuming work
- People having symptoms of fever, cough, vomit, diarrhea, etc. should be directed to not resume work without proper joining advice/fitness certificate from the Medical Officer. Details of such employees to be shared with unit head at units and Head of Department at Head Office and company doctor
- Every employee and out-sourced staff should register himself/herself in "AAROGYA SETU" mobile application, developed by Government of India for proper information and awareness about COVID-19.
- Fumigation of the entire premises, employee transport, forklifts/stackers and other critical areas, washrooms, toilets, canteen, hand wash areas etc.
- No physical meetings. Strictly adhere to the social distance of minimum 1 meter. Avoid hard copy files/papers to the extent possible. No Biometric Attendance

Every day after coming back home, the first thing was to sanitize his hands. He used to take a bath and wash the office dress - an additional burden after a tiring day in the office. The most emotionally disturbing was his inability to hug his dear son on returning home even when the innocent little creature was insisting so. His son was suddenly stopped forcibly by his mother to do so. Immediate query from the kid was, "Papa no more loves me." Strange behavior and SOP were emotional torture for the little heart.

His wife was working in an IT company as a program developer. She was allowed to 'work from home'. There were rumors of retrenchment in her company and that was one of the reasons for another tension in the house. Since both of them were working, they used to earlier put Rajan in a baby sitter's house nearby. The fear of coronavirus had stopped that too. Mother could not entertain her child while busy with the official work at home. Tired of all these, she once offered her husband to resign from her IT job. But the pressure of the payment of heavy housing loan instalment every month stopped her from doing so. The dilemma did not last much, since just next month she got retrenchment notice. A mixed feeling of freedom to take care of her lovely child but the financial pressure was making things complicated resulting into frequent fights between the couple. We, as a close neighbor, were just silent spectators.

The other next-door neighbor was a bright young man of 35, Mr. Abhijeet Sen, a Senior Vigilance Officer in the reputed Bank of India. I used to envy him. He got a senior entry level post in the bank at such an early age of 23. Getting such a seniority at the age of 35 is rare. He had a beautiful wife and a cute 6 years old daughter. Handsome salary, a lavish bungalow, high end car and professional success, all seemed to be a dream come true for a person of his age. Nonetheless, it had a dark side too. It is well said that 'maturity matters.' With high posts comes high responsibility. He was too burdened with the workload to handle it at such a tender age where the tricks and trivialities of life were yet to ripen. An honest and innocent man, he was also a man of conscience. In most offices, usually burden is assigned to those who take burden. Abhijeet by nature never learned to say no. Seniors as well as juniors used to take advantage of this nature. Slowly he started to become alcoholics with the side effect of lessening attention to his wife and daughter. Intermittent altercation between husband and wife was a common thing. The little initial bickering turned into major fights with increasing frequency. I was so friendly to him that I used to feel the pain of their suffering. Many times, I voluntarily was counselling but of no avail. His poor little dolly was totally confused and bemused. The couple used to fight practically every day.

Abhijeet, on weekends, was meeting me and used to murmur, "I cannot handle so much work at the office. Even my boss does not understand me. He just says, it is part of the job and I have to complete the responsibility commensurate to the job chart."

I just tried to pacify him, "Learn to say no and get ready for consequences. Face it bravely. Every problem in this world has a solution. I am sure things will be straightened out."

"Come on man. It is not that easy. You know the worst part is that even my wife does not understand me. She is too demanding to handle. How can I sustain the work pressure and tension at home too?" he retorted.

He further continued, "This bloody Covid-19 had to come now only. With only 30% staff in office, the workload has further multiplied. I am finding it unbearable day by day. Moreover, the vigilance duty is such that you need to be tricky, liar and ruthless. Where from, should I attain such so-called qualities? Recently another psychological problem I am facing. Every day, in one corner of mind, I feel I will contract coronavirus due to regular and unavoidable public contact. My family and especially my little daughter will die due to me."

The inevitable happened one day when I heard frantic wailing of his wife. I presumed that they were again fighting and as I kept climbing the staircase to their first-floor shouting at them, "Stop fighting man. Can't you live in peace even for a single day?" and entered the upper courtyard. The scene before me was so frightening that I felt for a moment my whole body frozen. Abhijeet was hanging with his neck choked with a rope tied on a pipeline of his upper floor water tank. His body was still and cold, naturally meaning that he was dead. But we had to try our best to resuscitate him. With the help of his wife, we brought down his body to the floor. I called on the emergency number 100. Within 10 minutes, police with an ambulance and doctor reached. The doctor immediately declared him dead. This was the indirect casualty of Covid-19.

His family were living far away in Kolkata. It would take a day for them to arrive. Till that time, I was the only help. What a dilemma? Covid-19 protocol prohibited any public contact and on the other hand was such a situation that I had to help them. For a moment I forgot that it was an unprecedented coronavirus situation. My family members were worried but we had no choice. I was involved in all the formalities and paperwork running around like his own brother. His relatives reached by evening but his wife was reluctant to entertain them. This was another disturbing situation. Finally, we got their relatives to stay with us. We requested them to follow all SOP for coronavirus. But they were so careless that this created tension in my house. Even in the grieving situation, we had to shout at them to maintain the SOP. Needless to say, that we were fully exposed to the pandemic. They stayed for three days and finally we bid farewell to his wife and the unruly relatives. We had a sigh of relief but with a fear inside of contracting coronavirus. We decided to get ourselves checked with our family doctor and called him. The doctor with a cautious voice informed that he was not in the city and had closed his clinic for some time. However, he suggested few measures to be taken. This was shocking for my family since we had a blind faith in our family doctor. Even he was scared of coronavirus. Finally, we contacted the designated government doctor for this area. He heard us patiently and appreciated our support to the bereaved family. Some symptomatic diagnosis was done along with some blood tests. Finally, all the family members were found corona negative. We were thinking disgustingly, "How many more the coronavirus adverse impact will have on our lives?" Let me remind you that these were just indirect impacts of coronavirus pandemic.

The experts of pandemic had a strong observation and the same was also touched upon in the national address by the Prime Minister that senior citizens with the age of more than 60 and the persons with history of comorbidity of serious ailments were more vulnerable to Covid-19. That was the worry for us since my senior citizen parents were retired and had a history of diabetes and high blood pressure. The experts also had an interesting observation that senior citizens were not in general taking the pandemic seriously. Many of them are acting as stubborn children. Same thing happened in my house.

My father is a religious person. Every second Sunday he used to have meetings with like-minded senior citizens wherein they used to discuss the life philosophy. He used to enjoy it since this was giving lots of food for thought and a spiritual serenity. Such a congregation was organized in turn in the houses of members. Just after the incidence of Abhijeet, the turn came to our house. Papa had a strong feeling that coronavirus will have no impact on any act of spirituality. Ultimately God is the savior. For me it was utter foolishness. I even told him that even temples, churches, mosques and gurdwaras are closed and no congregation was allowed as per government orders.

Even then his arguments continued, "Son! Our every breath is in the hands of God. If you are supposed to die you cannot survive even for a second and if you are supposed to survive, no eventuality will kill you. Let us not stop our communion with God." he was adamant.

I argued back, "Then why do you take medicines for your diabetes and high blood pressure? Just stop it and God will save."

"This is to keep my body fit but my soul is as enlightened as ever. Moreover, the participants are from good families. They maintain hygiene and cleanliness. All of them will come with masks and gloves. We will maintain a safe distance of 1 meter from each other. After the meeting, they will just have their meal and will leave." he said, not in a mood to listen to me.

My immediate reaction was, "I and the rest of the family members do not agree with you. We are scared."

Now was the time for him to be assertive, "This is my house. I will do whatever I want. Nobody has the right to stop me."

I don't know what happened to me suddenly. Within a minute I got mad. My survival instinct was coming to the fore. I was so worried for the old parents. My both ears were red, face tense and my fingers convulsively clenched into fists. I did not know what to do with this adamant and stubborn old man. I forced a blow on his face and started frantically shouting, "Let anybody come to my house. I will kill him with the iron rod kept in the kitchen. Nobody will enter my house till the pandemic situation is not over. Do you want the meeting? Organize it. I will see how it happens."

My father was shell-shocked. In India, with a joint family system, still father is the authority and his words are final in any proceedings of the house. I was directly challenging his authority. For a moment he was dumb-founded and after taking a deep breath shouted back, "What are you telling my house, my house, my house? This is my house. Just get out of my house. I don't want to see your face anymore."

My mother was shivering with shock and tried to pacify me, "Cool down son. This is very bad. You should not have hit him." I pushed my mother in the rage and she fell down on the floor, although slowly. My father ran to save her.

My verbose continued targeting my father, "Can you see! Just she fell down a little and you could not tolerate it. What if she contracts coronavirus in your so-called bloody useless congregation? Will you be happy then? And let me tell you I am not going anywhere whether you like it or not. You are the man who spoiled my life and I am not going to spare you."

Mother was ultimately successful in separating us in different rooms. I cooled down in a few minutes pondering what had suddenly happened to me. I had deep respect for my father. I could never imagine that I would hit him ever. Father finally agreed after my mother's persuasion that the meeting should be postponed. But the scar he got in his wounded heart was not ready to heal. A man deeply hurt by the acts of his loved one was the dichotomy he was struggling with and that transpired into a sharp rise of his blood pressure. We always wanted to avoid going to any hospital due to pandemic scare. He suddenly got up and started his car to go to nearby Inlaks and Budhrani Hospital. I was totally unaware and asked my mother, "Where is he going?" Mother said he was having his BP very high and suddenly got up and went to hospital to consult the specialist. "Has he taken his mask and gloves?" I enquired and was relieved to get the answer in affirmative.

A kind of guilt was killing me. I sent a message to his mobile phone while he was in the hospital, "Papa. I am really sorry. I did not know what had happened to me. I was totally out of my mind. I was very scared deeply in my heart and never wanted my nears and dears to get affected by coronavirus. It will never happen again."

He came back saying that the doctor had given some medication assuring that he was out of danger. In a remote corner of mind all of us were worried that he might have contracted coronavirus in the hospital. Thank God. Nothing untoward happened. Whatever may be, he was still hurt deeply. He did not reply to my message. We were not on talking terms. While passing by his room I saw him crying in the lap of my mother. Everything was so disturbing. Life had suddenly become burdened. My mother told me later that he was more perplexed, how could he spoil my life that I blamed him the other day. My elder brother was just a mute spectator. The dilemma for him was that both of us were either right or wrong. However, he did not want to meddle with any of us expecting that everything will get settled with time.

On the seventh day after the unruly incident, I got a message on my mobile phone from my father,

"Since you have sent me in writing, I am replying in writing. I am still in shock of the blow and trying to recover. Allow me some time to come to my terms and to become normal. You know it is not easy when one gets such things from so close. The turbulent thoughts are killing me hence I hope you won't mind allowing me to express my feelings. The issue is much deeper than you saying sorry and I forgiving you. I know it was not totally your fault. You were not under your control. It was a surge of anger. Yes, you were mainly scared that I should not get affected by corona by some outsider visiting our home followed by the whole family getting infected. Finally, the intention was good. Leave apart the violent reactions and resulting verbose."

"What I want to put forth is something else. You have deeply etched in your mind that I have spoiled your life and I am mainly responsible for all your troubles. I was shouting at you and sometimes beating you in your childhood mainly so that you can be successful in your life by being serious like your brother. Your careless attitude towards your study and career was disturbing me like anything. Maybe I was wrong since now you are successful even with all your negligent attitude in childhood. My intention was good. Now I realize that context of life is more important than content. Hence, I am proud of you for all your success. I am sure you will come out in flying colors in future too. At least you can forgive me now."

"Let us accept that we have in our family the problem that we are somewhat schizophrenic. Only the extent varies. It might have come from genes. I had heard that the elder brother of my grandfather had uncontrollable anger due to which the whole city was scared. My elder brother (a successful writer) also had a similar problem but he never realized or accepted it. The problems are only at a low level. Say if I have the problem 10%, you have a little more say 20%. Many times, even I feel a similar surge. Anyway, this cannot be said to be at disease level. It is just dis-ease. There is no medicine for it. We have to manage it with self-suggestions. I am so proud of you that you have successfully managed it so long. You know how worried I was for you during your adolescence. Many highly successful and famous personalities in the past had such problems which they managed very well."

"The problem will remain there till you consider that you parents (and specifically me) are responsible for your troubles. I will remain a trigger point for you any time we will have even a little heated discussion. I want you to believe that we love you so much that we can never be a hurdle in your life. Suppose your firm belief otherwise is still there, then we need to keep away from each other to avoid the occurrence of trigger point. Let the corona problem subside and I will make a sincere effort to keep away from you so that you can live happily."

"After the last incident a few days back, I was constantly crying. I was thinking of somehow hurting you to take revenge. Finally, by analyzing thoroughly I confessed to your mother that basically I love you a lot and that is the root cause of myself feeling deeply hurt and confused. In the fit of anger if I hurt you, the pain will be inflicted on me only. The moment I realized this; the peace descended on me. Maybe after my death you will realize how much I love you since the real value of a person is known only when he is no more. We had a series of misunderstandings. You might think of me as a devil. I do not care as long as I am honest. Both of my children are gifts of God to me. How can one smash his own lovely gifts?"

It was my turn to take initiative. I allowed a full month till his wounded heart got somewhat healed. I said one day, "Papa the dinner is ready. Mom is calling us. Would you like to share the dinner table with us?" He looked at me with a blank eye and just said, "Yes." I knew that the spring was in the offing after a rough winter. Once again, the Covid-19 was the main anchor in the whole family drama of ugly face.

Meanwhile we got a phone call from my cousin sister that her daughter needs to get married since her engagement was already performed January 2020 before the corona scare started in March. She was supposed to get married in the month of April. However, it was not possible due to covid-19 situation. The bridegroom's family were insisting that the marriage ceremony must be performed at the earliest since the boy had to report to his duties as doctor at the reputed hospital in the capital city and he did not want to live alone. My sister was inviting us albeit hesitantly. In pre Covid-19 days we could have been the happiest to join the celebration. But now everybody was skeptical.

Just last year we attended the marriage ceremony of my cousin brother's daughter. Total 30 families of relatives were present for pre- to post- wedding ceremonies. What a great family get-together it was! Everybody was in a celebratory mood. I prefer, on such occasions, to mingle up with a kid's group that makes me always feel younger and energetic. I collected all the kids with age groups from 5 to 15 years in one spare room and we decided to cut jokes, sing songs and perform dance. One of them was having a guitar to support the singers. They sang beautiful songs and danced. Some of them performed stand-up comedy. My turn was to say a joke. I was ready but with a condition that once they like it all of them must shout it out 'Yaa..hoo' and they agreed.

I started with a soft tone:

In north India, there is a place called Lucknow where people are very courteous. Some of them are over courteous. They prefer to undermine their achievements or accolades out of courtesy. A gentleman from another city totally oblivious of such things came to settle in Lucknow for the first time. One of his friends invited him for dinner. The moment he entered his beautiful and well decorated house he said, "Welcome to my little hut." The guest was surprised that the host was calling his such a nice house as a little hut. Some time passed. Delicious and sumptuous dinner was served. The host again started, "Welcome to dinner. These are the simple and plain food, whatever possible we serve you, my friend." Another shock to the guest! The guest's son had gone out for some work and he entered the house just as the dinner was to be served. The host uttered in his raised voice, "Great. You are there at the right time sonny. Meet our guest." Then he turned towards the guest, "This is the humble son of a poor guy like me." The third shock was unbearable and the host immediately asked the guest, "Why do you present everything in low key?" The self-deprecating host shot back, "This is a typical culture of Lucknow." The guest was satisfied now. Next was his turn to invite today's host. He did all the preparations and the moment his Lucknow friend arrived he was presenting himself as a meek host with folded hands for 'Namaste' and bent extra like Japanese. In a modest manner he murmured, "Welcome to my toilet like home." Later dinner was served and he politely said, "Welcome to dinner. These are the garbage, whatever possible we serve you, my friend." He had already instructed his son to enter the house the moment dinner was being served. His son entered as planned and he shouted, ""Great. You are there at the right time sonny. Meet our guest." Then he turned towards his Lucknow friend, "This is my bastard son."

Needless to say, that the kids group burst into laughter and as promised the tumultuous shout of 'Yaa..hoo..' was reverberating in the whole building and the impact was so loud that all the relatives started gathering around us in curiosity.

Alas! That was not to happen this time. We flatly refused to join the marriage ceremony of my cousin sister's daughter. She was sad but understanding. Finally, the marriage ceremony was performed on June 25. Who could have imagined that even the marriage ceremony of people so close to our heart would be attended through online live streaming? Our eyes were fixed on the TV screen throughout the marriage proceedings missing the loved ones. Only 10 persons from each side of the groom and bride were allowed to attend. All decorations, lightings and buffets were lackluster without the intermingling guests. This is how the celebrations were corona-ized.

Meanwhile a government order was issued that the registrations of all the general medical practitioners would be cancelled if they do not start their private clinics by the first week of August. As a result, my family doctor resumed his duties. Before this he was just providing services through video conferencing or photographs sent as WhatsApp messages. We used to pay his fees online using BHIM UPI developed by Govt. of India. We needed him since I developed pain in my stomach. There was no way out but to visit him. We visited his clinic which was practically deserted. Most of the people in society were postponing getting sick. This was one of the positive aspects of the pandemic, otherwise earlier for every small issue visit to a doctor was a fashion. The clinic was fully disinfected and fumigated. The doctor was fully covered in a PPE kit. He instructed me to sit at a distance and after asking details, prescribed medicines. No stethoscope, no physical check-up, just a remote OPD. I paid him online. No cash handling. I was prepared with my mask and gloves before check-up. The readers can see now. How even a simple life had become complicated?

Just when I arrived at home, we received a phone call from our cousin from our native place. He was sobbing inconsolably and reported that my grandmother had died. My father was stunned, tears rolling over his cheeks unstoppable. Our native place in Gwalior is around 1000 km from Pune. He insisted on seeing his mother on her last journey even while taking risks. We enquired; and found no flights or trains available. Further detailed talks with my uncle clarified that there was no point in going there since grandmother had died of coronavirus. Nobody was allowed to see her body. Even my uncle was allowed to see her face only through the glass window. My uncle works in JK Tyre Company, Gwalior. Although it was working with minimum staff, my uncle's presence was mandatory. Every day he had to attend the office. He was unaware of the fact that regular exposure to the public had exposed him to coronavirus. He contracted the virus but it was asymptomatic. Even my aunt and cousin had contracted coronavirus but all asymptomatic. It was only when grandmother fell sick, they contacted the doctor who suggested to get a proper test of coronavirus done and to utter shock to them, all of them were infected. As regards my grandmother, comorbidity had taken her life since she already had so many health complications. The hospital did not even allow to hand over the dead body to the family members. They disposed it off at their own level. Whole family of my uncle was hospitalized for treatment. Nobody was ready for such an eventuality. It was so frustrating and extremely painful for all of us that an eerie silence prevailed in our house. We never had imagined that coronavirus would affect our family directly.

Coronavirus had impacted all walks of our lives. Another cousin sister of mine was stuck at her son's house at Bhopal for one and half months. It was urgent for her to come back to Mumbai. Finally, the central government allowed limited flights with a defined SOP to be followed. She came by flight like a prisoner to Mumbai. Every step was a hurdle: Not allowed to touch anything, use sanitizer regularly, maintain safe distance, trolley not allowed, etc. Worst was to sit in a fully protected PPE for the whole flight duration of one and half hours. It was very uncomfortable.

My father's sister staying locally in Pune is emotionally very close to him. She used to earlier visit him every 15 days and was feeling restless to meet him. We purposely avoided her inflicting a great pain to her. I think it was the first time in my life when even close relatives were not welcome. It was an odd experience for my professor friend in Pune when he was asked by his college to conduct regular online classes. Personal interaction with students had a different impact. Slowly he got used to it but half satisfied. The main hurdle was that experiments in the laboratory could not be conducted without which the teaching was incomplete. How can you produce real engineers without practical classes? Daily walking of my parents which was must as recommended by his doctor discontinued. They used to walk in the house only from one room to the other. Lack of exposure to sun was causing vitamin D deficiency. For me and my brother, going to the gym was out of question. We joined online yoga classes. It was better than nothing. We avoided going to grocery and vegetable shops since no safe distance norm was maintained there even after frantic appeal by the government authorities. Hence, we did practically all the shopping online for our daily requirements. The delivery boys were not supposed to touch our call bell. They used to call us and we opened the door in advance. We kept a separate tub near the main door where they dropped the supply materials. We were allowing the materials to remain there for a minimum of 24 hours before using them. Even while using the grocery, outer packets were sanitized. Vegetables were dipped in mild chlorine water before use.

All the malls and movie theatres were closed. They were suffering from huge losses. Many jobs were lost. We were not supposed to touch newspapers. Lack of entertainment with no outing had given us the feeling of living under house arrest. Practically we had not ventured out from our house for 60 days at a stretch. It was an online life: online shopping, online streaming, online banking transaction, online payments, online office work, online medical support, online marketing and what not. Maybe in the future we would experience online sleeping, online dreaming, online bathing, online breathing and what not. Corona O Corona! When will you end your subpoena?

Before we end this section, let us have a bird's eye view of news, views and reports on impact of coronavirus in addition to my direct experience. I wonder if there is any positive impact too.

"Every second Indian hit by Corona anxiety" was the heading of Times News Network (TNN), India reported by Durgesh Nandan Jha on September 16, 2020. According to them this could be a silent epidemic of its own. A survey conducted by Max Healthcare, Saket, New Delhi revealed, one in every four persons is so stressed that he or she actually requires medical intervention since the idea of self-harm or death had crossed their mind at least once and 3% reported having such thoughts repeatedly. Every second Indian shows some signs of anxiety.

Another report entitled "The Implications of COVID-19 for Mental Health and Substance Use" published on https://www.kff.org/ by Nirmita Panchal et.al. dated Aug 21, 2020 revealed detailed implications of the epidemic. Their observations highlight that many adults are also reporting specific negative impacts on their mental health and wellbeing, such as difficulty in sleeping or eating, increase in alcohol consumption or substance use, and worsening chronic conditions, due to worry and stress over the coronavirus. As the pandemic wears on, ongoing and necessary public health measures expose many people to experiencing situations linked to poor mental health outcomes, such as isolation and job loss. Mainly job loss and income insecurity were associated with increased depression, anxiety, distress, and low self-esteem that may lead to higher rates of substance use disorder and suicide. Mental health disorders were common comorbidities among patients with chronic illnesses. Very little is known about mental health associated with coronavirus and substance use. Emotional toll due to burnout among health care providers was another field of urgent medical attention. Current shortage of mental health professionals further add fuel to the fire.

"Coronavirus triggers a mental health crisis in India" was the topic discussed by Aditya Sharma on July 01, 2020 on https://www.dw.com/. According to him India's coronavirus crisis has pushed millions into forced isolation and unemployment. Health experts warn that anxiety, depression and suicide are on the rise and that mental health could be the country's next crisis. A recent survey by the Indian Psychiatry Society (IPS) found that the number of mental illness cases had increased by 20% since the lockdown, and that at least one in five Indians were affected. Adolescents were the worst affected due to missed career opportunities, lost sessions and cancelled competitive examinations. Psychiatrists warned that children were at particular risk of developing mental health problems as a result of the pandemic, citing forced isolation and increased levels of family violence during the lockdown as detrimental to their wellbeing. People went into unplanned alcohol withdrawal which ultimately led to a cluster of suicides. This was an India-specific feature.

Mental illness problems were observed in the initial 2-3 months itself. A report on https://www.rfi.fr/ published on 14/05/2020 highlighted many cases of suicides in India due to lockdown effect. Nelson Vinod Moses of the Suicide Prevention India Foundation had the apprehension, "Rural India may be particularly susceptible to suicide due to the influx of migrant workers, and also because it is home to the at-risk farming community."

Nobody could have imagined that even international border tension could be the indirect impact of coronavirus. Whole world was blaming China for being responsible for the spread of Covid-19 from their laboratory and all countries are suffering due to this negligence. China had a fear of backlash from the international community. So, the best way was to create distraction and that they did successfully. They purposely started clashes in south china sea, at Japan border and in Taiwan air space. They perceived India as the softest target and hence effected incursion on eastern border of Ladakh. The simmering tension for months resulted in physical blows between the two armies. Twenty Indian Army personnel, including a Colonel, were killed in a clash with Chinese troops in the Galwan Valley on June 15, 2020. The Chinese side suffered casualties of 43 Chinese soldiers (including the death of an officer). The Economic Times reported on June 19, 2020 with the heading of "Chinese acts on India border meant to take advantage of COVID distractions: US official." According to them, Assistant Secretary for East Asian and Pacific Affairs David Stilwell made the remark, "China opening multiple fronts like the one on the border with India is because of Beijing's assessment that the world is "distracted" due to the COVID-19 pandemic and it could take advantage of it."

India Today Web Desk, New Delhi on September 12, 2020 suggested some useful tips to common people for how to tackle the situation. Some ways to deal with social isolation were:
- Don't be ashamed of being anxious or any mental health issue as all of us are in this together
- Keep yourself occupied and Schedule your day according to the day's responsibilities both professionally and personally.
- Keep yourself involved in household chores and simple indoor exercises to keep yourself active that will eventually improve your mental fitness as well.
- Consume nutritious food: fresh, fibrous and nutritious food and drink plenty of fluids.
- Step away from social media and news which may trigger your mental health.
- Exercise empathy and kindness to elder people and help them in whichever way possible.
- Connect with your friends and dear ones who can help you express more and relax your mind.
- Use this isolation to work on yourself, your mental health issues.

Positive Impact of Coronavirus:

From various corners we gathered the surprising observations that coronavirus had a positive impact too. Let us find some of them:
- You explored real friends and genuine relationships who support you morally, physically and monetarily during tough times.
- Government's SOP (Standard Operating Procedures) on preventive measures to contain the spread of COVID-19 had

become a way of life to practice better hygiene leading naturally to good health.

- People had become more communicative to stay connected with nears and dears, out of a caring attitude.
- Education had become digitized and affordable using a new wave of tools and software.
- Virtual office spaces and work from home had become a new norm in businesses, helping them to reduce office infrastructure cost to a great extent.
- Real estate in most of the cities, especially metros, had become affordable due to vacated offices and rented residential apartments.
- Fewer cars on roads resulted in much less pollution and blue skies to breath fresh air even in dense areas.
- Nobody wanted to get sick, thus avoid going to doctor for minor health problems, being more health conscious to have nutritional food and maintaining exercise regime.
- Lesser accidents had been the most remarkable observation of the transport department which proved that in the initial months of complete lockdown, the number of deaths due to coronavirus was much less that those of road accidents in the similar period last year.
- For the national economy, the best part was that the country for the first time focused on self-reliance and the new slogan of 'Vocal for Local' was doing the rounds.
- Internationally due to lack of demand, prices of fuel fell to record levels resulting in great relief to fuel users.
- There was a definite fall in crime rate graph due to homebound population and enhanced police vigilance.
- It was a great relief to wildlife with lesser population pressures. You could see peacocks, deer, nilgai or blue bulls roaming around the erstwhile busy malls and city centers.
- A new culture of global digital transformation and fast-tracking was happening due to non-cash online payments, online shopping and online doctor consultations.
- Restructuring of five million jobs was reported introducing new job charts and designations through innovative human resource activities.
- Compulsory wearing masks for everybody was enforced to keep his mouth shut. No more 'argumentative Indians' as despised earlier by the Nobel laureate Amartya Sen.
- Male dominated society first time learnt cooking, vegetable shopping, housekeeping and washing utensils since entry of all

domestic helps were banned completely from many housing complexes.

- The intangible benefit of spiritual orientation was of no less importance. For some, better stress management using Yoga and philosophical gratification using YouTube videos was a lifetime achievement.
- Closure of large malls helped small utility stores back into the limelight which is good for micro-management of the economy.
- With closed movie theatres and opera houses, home theatre with homely comfort and quality family time was a great family bonding force.
- Interestingly, a joke was doing the rounds that Corona's CV would look better than that of many CEOs!

Meanwhile daily corona cases were drastically reduced after October 2020 and lowest per day cases were reported in the first week of February 2021. The whole country was relaxed and enjoyed the freedom of movement once again. Good news was that the vaccines were now available namely Covishield and Covaxin. Covaxin has been developed by Hyderabad-based Bharat Biotech International Ltd in association with the Indian Council of Medical Research (ICMR) and the National Institute of Virology (NIV). Covaxin is an inactivated vaccine which means that it is made up of killed coronaviruses, making it safe to be injected into the body. Bharat Biotech used a sample of the coronavirus, isolated by India's National Institute of Virology. On the other hand, Covishield has been developed by the Oxford-AstraZeneca and is being manufactured by the Serum Institute of India (SII). The vaccine is made from a weakened version of a common cold virus (known as an adenovirus) from chimpanzees. Efficacies of the two types of vaccines also were well proven by a series of pretesting and have got proper government approvals. India launched its vaccine drive, the world's largest inoculation effort, in early January. It had vaccinated nearly 30 million healthcare and frontline workers on priority in the first phase. By the first week of February 2021, people over 60 and those who were between 45 and 59 but have other illnesses were getting vaccinated. Meanwhile there were reports of blood clotting in the persons getting Covishield in European countries. But it was not a general case and no such case was observed in India and hence was declared safe finally. My parents took the first shots of Covishield in the second week of February 2021. As a normal side effect, they had mild fever which was taken care of by taking paracetamol for two days. The third day they were fine. The second shot was given between 12 to 15 weeks. Thus, India rolled out the world's largest COVID-19 vaccination drive and by July 2021 a record 430 million of the population had got at least first shot. We felt great relief after struggling with the Covid-19 scare for more than one year.

As the country got relieved and relaxed, elections in four states were declared. This resulted in a large scale of gatherings during canvassing rallies. Other states had the common public lax in not using masks and freely moving in crowded areas. An obvious outcome was the second wave of surge of Covid-19 cases starting the second week of March 2021. The government accelerated the vaccination process and Covid-19 accelerated its growth taking advantage of people's lazy approach. The hide and seek game were in progress. Experts said that this rollercoaster would continue for some years till the graph is flattened. Some of them predicted second wave of Covid-19 which may be more dangerous due to callous attitude of general public. After all, the man has to win. Gone are the days of helplessness.

My encounter with coronavirus

If you recall my harrowing experience of the Hospital Corona Corner, in the first chapter, I was hospitalized there in the month of October, 2020.

In general, we were proud to have such a reputed hospital just within 500 meters from my house. A great relief and safety were felt by the dwellings in its vicinity since the hospital belonged to a reputed group of companies namely Powar Healthcare Services Private Limited. They were the owners of a series of hospitals and other healthcare services headed by its chairman Mr. Y. K. Powar who was also a political stalwart and was well respected by all the political fraternities from state to central governments. Besides running the commercial hospitals, he also ran a few not-for-profit hospitals too for the underprivileged ones; leading to many national civil awards accorded to him. A blind trust by the public to him and his institutions were the forte that helped him achieve many socio-political accolades.

I had developed the symptoms of simple cough and cold. We waited for a few days but the fever was persistent and that cautioned us not to take it as a simple common cold. Our family doctor also suggested that I should get the corona test done. The nearest hospital "Corona Corner" was the best to consult according to our family members. After my hospitalization, I gave my swab sample and within 2 days they confirmed it to be positive. In the first consultation itself they started creating emergencies taking advantage of our confused mental state. We wanted a second opinion and second confirmatory test from any other laboratory since I was not feeling any other complications such as weakness, breathlessness, loss of smell, loss of appetite, etc. But I was surprised to watch their hurrying attitude. The doctor on duty suggested that I first remain admitted and then take a second opinion or blood test. He promised that they would allow outside medical consultants to visit their hospital. As stated in the first chapter, this was proven wrong later, since they were maintaining utter secrecy and won't allow outside doctors to enter their premises. Once you entered there, you were practically imprisoned with unusually tight security and dubious protocol to meet relatives. Since the beginning, I could sense some kind of mysterious activity.

Just after my escape from the shocking ordeal as stated in the first chapter, a massive police raid was conducted by the local police in-charge. The Superintendent of Police had a reputation of being a daredevil. Normally no police officer could have dared touch the hospital owned by a person of such a repute. However, this guy was clever enough to judge the situation and he very well knew that the earliest action was the need of the hour. He had a brief secret meeting of selected officers, got additional enforcement from a nearby police station and issued a clear instruction: "It is now or never. Sooner the better. Hit the iron while hot." Some of the police personnel were hesitant, fearing backlash from political bosses. But soon they were in action. This worked in my favor to expose the racket without anybody noticing me and my involvement since Mr. Powar was a very influential person and could have damaged my career as well as harming my family. Director of Hospital Corona Corner Dr Vivek Acharya along with 6 other staff members were arrested. The police team took very swift necessary actions to collect the proofs that could stand in judicial courts. Operation theatre was sealed. Hundreds of snaps were taken of many patients with removed organs, preserved organ banks and live operation theatre activities. All the accused were produced to the local judge and were sent to police custody for interrogation. Mr. Y. K. Powar was in New Delhi and he landed in Pune by evening the next day. His request to meet the accused was politely rejected by the Superintendent of Police. The case was of so prime importance considering its wider ramifications that the court decided to take the matter on priority. The hearing started within a week.

If you recall that the ward boy of my acquaintance had given me the mobile phone which was used by me to record photographs and audios in hiding. Just before returning to my hospital bed, I had sent these proofs to my mobile phone through WhatsApp. My mobile phone was kept safely in my cupboard while I was admitted to the hospital. The first thing I did after coming out of the servant's bathroom was to charge my mobile and retrieve these data on my laptop. I copied the data in a pen drive purchased from the roadside shop without any receipts. Next day I posted it as an unknown sender to the Superintendent of Police of the nearby police station. Another pen drive copy was sent to the city cable service who blew the lid with heavy pomp and show. His TRP (Television Rating Point) shot up in a day.

The defense lawyer was convincing Dr Vivek Acharya to deny their involvement and protect the interest and reputation of the institution. But God had different plans. Dr Acharya was filled with guilt and repentance. He had already watched the local city cable channel telecasting all his deeds. He decided to depose before the judge and say all the truth. His statements will go in history as one of the most moving stories of a man trapped in the duality of success and greed; describing the heinous crime by protectors of health and wellness. It was a glaring example of a constructor turning into a destructor. A large crowd was present every day on the days of hearings, witnessing the breach of trust by a social worker of very high reputation.

The public prosecutor Mr R M Pardeshi started in a low tone, "Can you tell your name and designation to the court?" He replied, "Dr Vivek Acharya, Director, Hospital Corona Corner." Mr Pardeshi asked, "Can you tell the court the details from the beginning?"

Dr Vivek Acharya started by clearing his throat, "My Lord. I plead guilty. I know that the case will be closed after me pleading guilty. But I want to tell the whole story so that all the people involved in it need to be exposed. I just want my family to be protected."

The judge instructed, "Dr Acharya, you can tell us all without any fear of repercussions. We assure you that your family will be protected."

Dr Acharya started, "I obtained my MBBS degree from the reputed P J Medical College, Pune. I have been an average student. Since the beginning, I was very ambitious and my main objective to obtain the medical degree was to earn lots of money. In my dreams many times I used to imagine myself as a billionaire and that attitude has landed me in the state where I am today."

Mr Pardeshi interrupted, "That is fine. The court would like to know about your involvement in this big racket of illegal human organ collection in the guise of coronavirus treatment. Can you tell us why you chose Corona treatment for such a crime?"

He replied, "It was easy. All kinds of mystery surround this new kind of virus. Nobody is aware of the course of treatment. Death can be easily proven natural due to this virus. Especially, the comorbid patients could be our easy targets and nobody would doubt us."

It was now the turn of Mr Pardeshi, "Well now you can tell us how it all started."

With a heavy sigh Dr Acharya continued, "Our company Powar Healthcare Services Private Limited always grabs any opportunity to start a new venture where possibility of large profit making is available. The whole world was struggling to counter the coronavirus danger in December 2019. We all knew that very soon India would be one of the most affected countries due to its dense population. Government hospitals might not be able to handle the situation on their own. Sooner or later, they would look for support from private hospitals. Wise are those who foresee the business opportunity much in advance. With this motto, we had a top-level meeting on 15 January 2020 comprising Mr. Y K Powar, myself, administrative officer and the company secretary of the group of companies. We had a general hospital namely Hospital Wellness Corner which was situated at the end of a lane in the south-west corner of the city. I was the Director of this hospital. It was not running very profitably probably due to the odd site situation. Mr Powar suggested it be renamed as Hospital Corona Corner and run it with all the latest facilities to tackle coronavirus patients. He was ready to invest INR 20 million to procure necessary equipment and accessories. A veiled warning was issued to us to recover this amount and then earn profit of at least three times of investment. We had no choice. All of us just agreed. Soon we rechristened the hospital as Hospital Corona Corner and purchased necessary equipment and kept it ready for the future use."

Public prosecutor interrupted, "Was it recognized by the state government for coronavirus treatment?"

"No. Not initially. We had a tough time with all the investments done. Fortunately, soon the pandemic started spreading fast and the government got alarmed. Mr. Powar had to influence the politicians at high level to announce the policy to involve private hospitals. Eventually the policy was announced that selected private hospitals can treat the Covid-19 patients and they would be compensated with finance of INR 200,000 per patient for full treatment. For other treatments such as quarantine, laboratory tests, etc. there were other financial packages provided. We were first to get recognition and registration. As a Director, I had now a target fixed to have at least 100 patients to recover the investment and then earn the profit." Dr. Acharya replied.

Mr. Pardeshi was quick to ask, "So could you make profit?"

Dr Acharya with downcast eyes muttered and then uttered, "That was the problem. That waaaas the problem Sir. The commercial pressure was killing us. By the end of July, we had been allotted only 28 patients till then. We had another confidential review meeting in the first week of August under the chairmanship of Mr. Powar. That changed the whole course. A criminal conspiracy was hatched out. We had another hospital dealing with human organs donation. Human organs were preserved there with all international standards. Most of the business was legal except for a few cases of grey market. Anyway, we had good contacts in the grey market fetching very high values for unregistered organ transplants. While donated organs have to be transplanted within 4-12 hours of recovery, tissue donations can be preserved and transplanted for up to five years. We decided to harvest organs from dead bodies and sell them in the grey market."

The judge intervened, "But you cannot do this without the consent of relatives of patients?"

"Yes, My Lord. But we took advantage of the grim situation. We inserted a sentence surreptitiously in the declaration form indicating no objection by the relatives for organ donations. We had two forms: one original to show to any inspecting government official and another of our use with inserted an extra clause. All the corona patients came to us in very bad mental states. They used to sign the form hurriedly without reading the details. Second point to our advantage was the SOP issued by the government. No relative was supposed to see the dead body with close proximity to avoid spread of the pandemic. They were allowed to see the patient only through a glass window. Also, the relatives were not allowed to take the body for cremation. It was to be cremated by us only. Hence it was very easy for us to extract the organs at the right time and pack the whole body fully to avoid any suspicion. The government inspectors were so bogged down with workload that they never suspected any foul play. Further, to make it foolproof, we were using a secret Russian technology to seal the dissected cuts on the body to look perfectly naturally intact." Dr Acharya deposed coolly.

"Were there any other illegal activities going on?" enquired the public prosecutor.

"Yes Sir. Many people used to approach us to get a negative coronavirus certificate before departing to other states or for flying to foreign countries. We were providing the negative certificate even without checking the collected blood sample. To hook patients, any one with even some symptoms of common cold-cough, we were declaring them corona affected even if they had negative test results. We used to create emergencies and admit such patients urgently. After administering normal medicines such as crocin for 10 days we were discharging them declaring them corona free. After all we were getting good compensation per patient from the government. To make extra money, some patients who even did not need to be put on a ventilator were done so. Worst was the case when we used to keep the patients on ventilators for a few days even when they were dead. Well, this practice is very common practically in all private hospitals too. In addition, overbilling was very common." said Dr Acharya

"What motivated you to take up such a heinous crime?"

Dr Acharya continued, "Let me agree that I was always a mediocre medical student in my classes. Even after getting the MBBS degree, I had no confidence that I would become a successful private practitioner. With my minimum credentials, getting a good job was also not an easy task. Being well connected to Mr Powar was the best qualification for me. Hence, I got a good administrative post with a handsome salary. But still my ex-college friends were doing much better financially and career wise. The craving for earning more was always there. Job insecurity never allowed me to leave this hospital. And then came the offer from this healthcare company to run this hospital commercially successfully. For carrying out the criminal activities I was given a huge commission per patient. That was enough to make me rich. All the core staff were compensated in a similar way and all of us were happy."

The public prosecutor asked, "What kind of patients were meeting this kind of ordeal?"

"We were mainly focusing on comorbid patients. In certain cases where patients were for prolonged periods on a ventilator, we used to carry out extraction of organs much in advance before their death.

Some young and healthy patients too met with such an ordeal when their health deteriorated with time. Let me clarify that under no circumstances, we used the organs of patients who were ready to get cured soon. There was not even a single purposely killing event. All were the natural death cases." was Dr Acharya's assent.

"How did you maintain secrecy so long till the month of November?" Mr Pardeshi shot back.

"We had a very tight security regime. Every staff and patient had to pass through three layers of security steps. Regarding our organ harvesting trade, only the top four staff members knew besides Mr. Powar. We were making it sure that the harvested organs were corona free incorporating the strict Covid-19 tests. This could help us make money without any hassle. Security personnel were strictly instructed not to allow any patient to go out without our permission. We had some doubt on some ward boys who were handling the body for final disposal. But we were not sure." Dr Acharya was now exhausted.

Based on the depositions of Dr Acharya, all the four hospital staff members were arrested along with the kingpin Mr Powar. All the electronic and print media were 24x7 busy with this news. Especially Mr Powar's arrest was very shocking to the society and political arena. Nobody had imagined such a thing from a philanthropic person of his repute.

At this point of time, I would like to refer to the news with the heading "The unravelling of a kidney racket" published in The Hindu a year back by B S Perappadan and S Trivedi dated July 27, 2019. With reference to the arrest of CEO of Pushpawati Singhania Research Institute (PSRI), Deepak Shukla and notices served to two leading doctors at Fortis Hospital in Delhi, they reported that:

"………The epicentre of this massive illegal organ trade is the National Capital Region. The web of criminals includes police personnel, doctors, hospital administration staff, medical support staff, and kidney and liver donors — all catering to patients with end-stage kidney and liver failure. These patients can't be treated with medicines or dialysis and therefore require a transplant. A dozen leading private surgeons are under the scanner now. These include top urologists in Delhi who allegedly worked in nexus with some police personnel from the Uttar Pradesh Police as well as brokers (some of whom were previous donors themselves) to ensure a smoothly running profitable trade, the value of which some people peg at over ☐100 crore. So far, 15 people, including the CEO of Pushpawati Singhania Research Institute (PSRI), Deepak Shukla, have been arrested, and notices have been served to two leading doctors at Fortis Hospital in Delhi for violation of the Transplantation of Human Organs (and Tissue) Act, 1994. This legislation was brought in with the objective of regulating the removal, storage and transplantation of human organs for therapeutic purposes and for the prevention of commercial dealings in human organs. These arrests and notices could prove to be only the tip of the iceberg. "Investigations against another leading hospital in central Delhi are currently under way and more arrests are likely," says a senior Delhi police officer who is investigating the case......"

The same news item described the status of human organs demand supply as follows:

"...........In 2016, in its reply to a Lok Sabha question, the Union Health Ministry noted that there is a huge gap between the demand and supply of human organs for transplant even though the precise numbers of premature deaths due to heart, liver, lung and pancreas failures have not been compiled. The Ministry noted that against the demand of 2 lakh kidneys, only 6,000 were available. Similarly, against the demand of 30,000 livers only 1,500 were available, and against the demand of 50,000 hearts merely 15 were available across the country. According to the Multi Organ Harvesting Aid Network Foundation (Mohan Foundation), a Chennai-based NGO working on organ donation, only about 3% of the demand is met. ....The industry is thriving despite several raids and laws against it because those who sell their organs are desperate for money. It is a trade that guarantees high profit. Plus, it's easy to do business in India......."

You can understand why this racket is flourishing in India. As regards the present case of Hospital Corona Corner, all the five convicts were found guilty for violation of the Transplantation of Human Organs (and Tissue) Act, 1994. They all got life sentences. Even their appeals to the higher courts were turned down.

The electronic and print media kept on digging further into the matter. All of them were vexed with the question of who threw the security guard down from the terrace of the hospital. Till today nobody knows.

I am still not able to come to terms that two security men were killed by me for their indirect involvement in the illegal organ trading. I had no choice. If I would not have killed them, I would have been killed finally on the pretext of coronavirus since I knew now their dirty secret. Probably some organs of my body could have been in the market for sale. I can just pray for their soul to be in peace. Only two of us, me and my father, know the secret. The most interesting thing is that me, the main whistleblower, will never be known to the world. I can see with muse, many articles in newspapers and news websites, wondering who killed the killers' network? Whatever it is, in one corner of my heart, there will always remain the 'Corona Corner'.

About the Author

Born in 1955 in a feudal family, Dr Sudhir Kumar has been a keen observer since his childhood. The sensitive intricacies of socio-economic interactions under the dichotomy of humanitarianism and authoritarianism have always intrigued him under the benevolent glow of universal love. Completely engrossed in the core of his soul, he wonders how the world moves with complacent slumber while being so active; at the same time, it creates a storm even in the eerie silence. Surprisingly for him, it appears that we all are somewhere-somehow every moment mobile under the guidance of an unknown inspirational aura. The sleep is an awareness and the awakening is a drowsiness. It appears that an author does not write; writing just happens. The spontaneity with which words flow in 'proses' like waves in a sacred river; the articulation with which rhythmical words spring up in 'poems' like a natural jungle stream, are the results of a meditative literary-weavers in a creative trance. A hidden bubbly child in Dr. Sudhir Kumar always wants to share a story with you. Just remain connected.

About the book:

"Corona Corner" is a classic example of a literature that reflects the inevitable impact of Covid-19 on our lives. Each of us has felt the direct or indirect implication of this pandemic to a certain extent. Never in the recent past, the world has felt so perplexed and vexed. The dangerous cocktail of confusion, helplessness, melancholy, loneliness, agony, irritation, frustration and rejection has poisoned each individual, transpiring into mental numbness. The worst thing was postponing the critical issues such as health problem, engagement, marriage, traditional festivals, meeting the loved ones; and more painful was not to attend the last rites of your close ones. An attitude was prevailing - "Let us first survive, then revive." It appeared that life would never be the same again. This book picturizes all these in the form of fiction to offer you a real-life experience.